Quest
for Lasting Love

Also by Jane Peart
in Large Print:

Dreams of a Longing Heart
Homeward the Seeking Heart
The Pattern
A Perilous Bargain
The Pledge
The Promise
The Risk of Loving
Shadow of Fear
Thread of Suspicion
Web of Deception

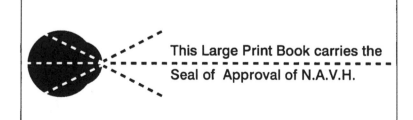

This Large Print Book carries the
Seal of Approval of N.A.V.H.

Quest
for Lasting Love

Jane Peart

Thorndike Press • Thorndike, Maine

Published in 2001 by arrangement with
Baker Book House Company.

Scripture quotations in this volume are from the
King James Version of the Bible.

Thorndike Press Large Print Christian Fiction Series.

The tree indicium is a trademark of Thorndike Press.

The text of this Large Print edition is unabridged.
Other aspects of the book may vary from the original edition.

Set in 16 pt. Plantin by Elena Picard.

Printed in the United States on permanent paper.

Library of Congress Cataloging-in-Publication Data

Peart, Jane.
    Quest for lasting love / Jane Peart.
        p. cm.
    ISBN 0-7862-3283-8 (lg. print : hc : alk. paper)
    1. Orphan trains — Fiction. 2. Large type books.
I. Title.
PS3566.E238 Q4 2001
813'.54—dc21   2001027026

To the *real* "riders" of the orphan trains, the over 100,000 children who were transported by train across the country to new homes in the Midwest, from 1854 to the early twentieth century, whose experience and courage inspired this series.

1

Boston
December 1888

Something dreadful was about to happen. Laurel just knew it. Mama had seemed strange all morning. In fact, Mama had not seemed like herself for weeks. Watching her mother move slowly about the small rooms they rented upstairs in Mrs. Campbell's big, dark house, Laurel was newly alarmed.

For weeks now, even when she was playing tea party with her dolls, Laurel often felt her mother gazing at her. When Laurel looked up, she would see a sad expression on the beautiful face, and the dark, violet-shadowed eyes would be glistening with tears.

Frightened, Laurel would ask, "Why are you crying, Mama?"

Then her mother would quickly gather Laurel up into her arms and hold her, saying, "Nothing, my darling. Everything will be all right, you'll see."

But things were not all right, Laurel knew, and day by day she could feel that little knot in her chest grow tighter. Something was wrong.

Her mother gave piano lessons on Tuesday and Thursday afternoons, and Laurel always played quietly in a corner of the room while the students fumbled through their scales and the simple pieces they never seemed to get quite right. Usually after the last pupil left, her mother would sit at the piano and play lovely, rippling melodies, filling the room with harmony. A welcome relief after two hours of missed keys and sour notes.

Lately, however, when the lessons were over, her mother closed the piano lid with a deep sigh. Then, pale and exhausted, she would lie down on the narrow sofa, one arm flung over her eyes. Laurel would come over and sit on the cushions behind her and gently stroke her forehead.

"What would I do without my little nurse?" her mother would say with a weary smile.

Sometimes she drifted into a shallow slumber, waking with a start, two bright spots of color in a face otherwise drawn and white.

"Oh, my, Laurel, our supper will have to be fashionably late this evening."

At mealtimes they pretended that the simple fare of bread, tea with milk, and a piece of fruit for Laurel was a sumptuous affair fit for royalty. Her mother would be Queen Lily and Laurel would be Princess Laura Elaine, which was her *real* "christened" name, after her two grandmothers.

Laurel did not know her grandmothers. Her mother told her that they both lived "a long way off," but someday she would meet them.

"Someday, when all is forgiven —" mother would murmur when Laurel asked when. Laurel did not understand. But she was so happy with the life they had together, she did not trouble herself with wondering about much else.

But more and more, things had been disturbingly different. She had awakened in the night several times to the sound of her mother's weeping — weeping that would often turn into a frightening paroxysm of coughing. Stiff with anxiety, Laurel, in her own small bed, would hug her doll Miranda. Hearing her mother get up, she would awaken to see her throw a shawl over her long, drifting nightgown and huddle in the chair by the window, trying to smother her hoarse racking cough.

It was one afternoon soon after a particularly bad night when the coughing had lasted a long time that her mother had left Laurel with Mrs. Campbell to go to the doctor.

Laurel liked staying with Mrs. Campbell, who was fat and jolly and cooked for the boarders who lived in her other rooms. She was usually in her large cheerful kitchen where she always seemed to be stirring something and where all sorts of wonderful things simmered on the stove, filling the air with delicious odors.

She pushed a little stool over for Laurel to stand on beside her at the big, square, scrubbed pine table and let her help roll out the biscuit dough. Then she showed her how to take a small glass tumbler, dip it into flour, and cut out the round shapes to be put on the baking sheet and placed in the oven of the big, black iron stove.

They were thus happily occupied when Laurel's mother returned. Mrs. Campbell took one look at her and pulled out her oak rocker for her to sit. Then she filled her blue kettle with water from the kitchen pump and placed it on the stove to boil.

"There now, rest a bit and I'll have a nice

cup of tea for you in a minute. You look that worn out, Lillian." Then in a lowered voice and with a furtive glance at the child, she asked, "Is it bad, then?"

Laurel's mother leaned her head against the high, fan-shaped back of the chair and nodded wordlessly. Laurel wiped her floury hands on the large apron Mrs. Campbell had tied around her, got down from the stool, walked over and climbed up into her mother's lap. Her mother nestled her close, resting her chin upon Laurel's soft dark curls, and answered Mrs. Campbell's question.

"Yes, Mrs. Campbell, very bad, indeed, I'm afraid. I shall have to make plans —" Her voice drifted away weakly.

"If there's anything I can do to help —"

There was something in Mrs. Campbell's response that made Laurel cuddle even closer to her mother, winding her little arms around her mother's waist, breathing in the sweet, violet scent of her. She felt an inner trembling. That dark thing she had felt hovering over them crept nearer.

Before she was even fully awake, Laurel heard the steady pattering of rain against the windows and felt her mother's hand gently stroking her hair.

"Come, darling, you must get up."

As Laurel sat up, sleepily rubbing her eyes, she saw that it was still dark outside.

"Is it nighttime?" she asked, watching her mother's slender figure moving about in the lamplight, setting the table for breakfast.

"No, precious, it is very early in the morning. But we both have to go somewhere, and I am fixing a special breakfast for us. Cocoa for you and the last of the coffee for me."

Even though her mother was being especially cheerful and gay, Laurel felt that queasy sensation stirring deep inside. Was this the day the dark unknown thing was going to happen?

The feeling was so strong Laurel could not really relish the surprise treat of sticky buns or the creamy hot cocoa.

But it wasn't until her mother had brushed her hair for an extra long time, carefully winding each curl around her fingers then tying them in bunches with velvet ribbons on both sides of her head, that she told Laurel what it was.

"You know, darling, Mama has not been feeling too well lately and the doctors tell me I must have a long rest if I want to get strong and healthy again. So, I have to go away to a place in the mountains where they can take care of me and help me get better. And you are going to stay at a nice place with a lot of other little girls and boys whose mamas are sick or away —" Here her voice broke and she hugged Laurel to her. Laurel felt the wetness of tears on her mother's soft cheek and she clung to her in sudden panic.

"But I don't want to go anywhere without you, Mama!"

"I know, my darling, but it will only be for a little while. I will come as soon as I can and get you and we will be together again. I promise!"

In stunned disbelief Laurel watched her mother pack a small valise with all her neatly ironed clothes — the dresses with the embroidered yokes, the pinafores, the white cotton chemises, panties, ruffled petticoats trimmed with crocheted edging, all handmade so lovingly for Laurel.

Then Lillian took off the gold chain and locket she always wore from around her own neck and fastened it around Laurel's.

"I want you to wear this until I come for you, Laurel." She pointed out the intertwined swirled letters on the heart-shaped front. "See these? They spell out our initials. The L.M. stands for Lillian Maynard — my maiden name — and the P.V. is for your father — Paul Vestal. It's important for you to remember that, Laurel," she said. "Your father gave me this before we were married, since he couldn't afford an engagement ring. But I always loved it." Then she opened the locket to show the pictures inside. One was of Lillian herself when she was a young girl with her dark hair falling in curls around her shoulders; the other picture, of a handsome, dark-eyed young man. "This is your precious papa, Laurel."

Laurel could not remember her father. He had been killed in a tragic accident, knocked down by a team of runaway horses when he was crossing the street on his way home one snowy evening when Laurel was just a baby.

"Now, remember, Laurel, don't take this off for any reason, until I come."

After that her mother buttoned her into her velour coat with the scalloped cape that she had fashioned for her only the month before. After she tied Laurel's satin bonnet strings under her chin, she kissed her on both cheeks. Then, hand in hand, they went quietly down the stairs of the sleeping house and out into the dark, rainy morning. At the street corner they found a cab and sad-looking horse, its driver bundled into a muffler, his chin on his chest, a battered stovepipe hat slipping forward on his brow.

Lillian squeezed Laurel's hand and said

with a hint of the old gaiety in her voice, "This is going to be quite an adventure, darling. As long as we have to go, we're going in style."

"Where to, lady?" The driver roused himself with a jerk.

"Greystone," Lillian told him as she helped Laurel mount the high, rickety steps into the cab.

"You mean the County Orphanage?" he barked.

"Yes," Lillian said and this time her voice quavered.

Inside, she put her arm around Laurel, drawing her close. The ancient gig swayed and jolted over the cobblestone streets through the dreary morning drizzle, jogging slowly up a steep hill. All the while, Laurel felt the chill creep in through the cracks of the old vehicle, into her very bones, and she shivered, leaning into her mother. They did not speak on the way, just clung to each other.

Finally the cab jerked to a stop in front of a stone fortress-like building.

The driver opened the roof flap and hollered down. "Greystone!"

Laurel's mother grasped her hand tightly and, after getting down herself, lifted Laurel down. Then she said to the cabbie. "Wait, please. I need to ride to the train depot."

15

Still holding Laurel by the hand, she mounted the steps. At the massive, double door, Lillian gave the metal doorbell a twist. Her mother was holding Laurel's hand so tightly it hurt her fingers, but even so she did not want to let go.

Finally the door was opened by a tall woman. She seemed to loom over them, making Laurel's mother seem smaller, more fragile than ever.

"Yes?" She regarded them with narrowed eyes, waiting for Laurel's mother to speak.

When it came, her voice seemed thin and faint. "I'm Lillian Vestal, I've come to. . . . This is my little daughter —"

"Ah, yes, Mrs. Vestal. We were expecting you." The woman stretched out her hand toward Laurel, who drew back. Then she spoke crisply to Laurel's mother. "It is best you leave now, ma'am. The children are at prayers and will be going into breakfast. There will be less of a fuss if you say goodbye here."

Laurel's hand clutched her mother's convulsively. She felt the sick rise of nausea into her throat. "No, no," she tried to say, but the words wouldn't come out.

Her mother bent to hug her, whispering, "You must be a brave, good girl, my darling. I will be back soon. Very soon."

"Come along, child." The voice in the doorway was firm.

Lillian pried Laurel's hands from around her neck, murmuring soothing words as Laurel felt herself being pulled out of her mother's embrace. She heard a smothered sob and turned to reach out again for her, but Lillian had already started down the steps.

At last she heard her own scream shrill through the air.

"Mama! Mama! Come back!"

At that moment Laurel was picked up bodily and thrust through the door. When she heard it slam behind her, she wriggled out of the confining arms that held her, flung herself sobbing against the thick impenetrable door, and pounded her tiny fists against it.

2

Greystone Orphanage

All her life Laurel would remember the bewildering change from her life with her mother to that at Greystone. Numbed with shock, she moved like a little sleepwalker, unconscious of the stares of the other children, the worried frowns of the orphanage staff. Unresponsive, she allowed herself to be placed in line for meals, but barely touched her food. Eyes lowered, she did not respond to friendly overtures, merely nodded yes or no if asked a direct question.

Only her big, dark eyes reflected the pain caused by the abrupt transfer from the small, warm, sheltered world she had shared with her adored mother to the large, impersonal institutional life of Greystone.

For the first two days Laurel was at Greystone, she got up in the morning at the rising bell like everyone else. Then she dressed, put on her coat and bonnet, went down the main stairway and planted herself on the bottom step, her arms folded across her chest, her mouth set stubbornly.

"My mother is coming for me," she stated flatly and shook her head at any request to come away. Miss Clinock wisely rejected the use of any disciplinary action on the part of the other matrons or having Laurel physically removed from her post.

On the third day, however, the Head Matron herself approached Laurel.

"Laurel, your mother left you with us while she is in the sanatorium getting well," Miss Clinock intoned. "But until then, she expects you to try to be happy here with the other children, to be obedient and do as you are told. Now, come along, Laurel," she said firmly and held out her hand. "You want us to give your mother a good report of you when she *does* come, don't you? You wouldn't want us to have to tell her you had been a naughty girl who wouldn't mind, would you?"

Tears turned Laurel's eyes into glistening coals. She didn't want Mama to be disappointed in her. Slowly she got up, lifting her chin bravely, but refusing to take Miss Clinock's outstretched hand.

"Come along, then, there's a good girl," the woman said and led the way upstairs to the third floor dormitory.

Rows of small iron cots lined the long room. Beside each bed was a small chest, on which was an enamel pitcher and washbowl. Next to that a wooden stool. As Miss Clinock entered with Laurel, two dozen heads turned and all the little girls momentarily stopped tidying their cubicles.

"Get on with your duties, children," Miss Clinock spoke crisply. Her eyes roved around the room, then spotted the one narrow cot left unmade, its blankets tossed back, the pillow rumpled. "Come along, Laurel," she said and made straight for that one.

"Kit," Miss Clinock addressed a girl with smooth brown braids, who was pulling up the covers of her own cot next to Laurel's. "Will you please show Laurel how to make her bed and put her clothes neatly away?"

The girl turned around, glancing at Laurel with a shy smile. "Yes, ma'am."

"Every morning before prayers and breakfast, Laurel, your bed is to be made, your nightclothes put away." Miss Clinock spoke directly to Laurel. "Starting today, you will wear the Greystone uniform like the rest of the girls in Third."

"But my *mother* made *my* clothes! She wants me to wear these," protested Laurel, her lower lip beginning to tremble.

"We will put the things your mother made

for you away carefully, Laurel, so that they will be ready for you when she comes. But while you are at Greystone, you will wear what the other girls wear," Miss Clinock said decisively.

Then she told Kit, "After things are put right here, Kit, take Laurel to Mrs. Weems in the Sewing Room to get a uniform." With that directive, the Head Matron left.

Laurel plumped down on the end of her cot, chin thrust out, arms folded again. She felt a gentle tug on the bedclothes underneath her as Kit began pulling them straight.

"Come on, I'll show you how. It's really easy," she said in a low voice.

A tear rolled slowly down Laurel's cheek. She didn't uncross her arms to free a hand to brush it away. Then she felt Kit's arm go around her shoulder. "I know how you feel," Kit whispered. "I felt the same way when I first came here. But you get used to it, honest."

"I'm not going to stay here," Laurel said as if trying to convince herself. "I don't have to. My mother is coming for me. *Soon!*" She squeezed both eyes shut tight, letting the tears flow unchecked.

"So is *mine!*" piped up a cheerful voice and Laurel opened her eyes to see a smiling little face with a tip-tilted nose pushed right up to hers, round blue eyes staring at her in-

21

quisitively. "Any day now." She reinforced her statement with a little nod and bounce as she popped herself down on the bed beside Laurel.

"And so is my *da*," chimed in Kit, adding her declaration to theirs. "At least, as soon as he gets a job."

The three looked at one another appraisingly. In that moment of mutual affirmation, some kind of bond was forged. As yet it had not been tested, but the foundation for friendship was laid. Each of them, in her desperate bid to believe that she was different from the other children at Greystone, found hope alive in at least two other hearts. By associating with the other two who also were determined to cling to that hope, her own was bolstered.

No three little girls could have been more different in appearance, personality or disposition, yet they became inseparable as the weeks turned into months and their status as "temporaries" inevitably changed.

If it had not been for the other two, Laurel would have found it even harder to adjust to Greystone. The overall drabness of the routine, the cheerless halls, the grinding daily routine of life was brightened a little for her by the companionship of Toddy and Kit.

The three sat at the same table at mealtimes, sought each other out during recreation. Kit was protective, shielding Laurel from some of the older children who were prone to bully the younger, shyer ones. Toddy, though small, was spunky and with her gift for mimicry often turned a potentially ugly playground incident into a comedy with herself as the clown.

During the weeks that followed, Toddy, Laurel and Kit grew closer. It was at night, when the lamps had been taken away, and she lay in her narrow little bed alone that Laurel felt most keenly the reality of her situation. Would her mama never come? she asked herself over and over, fingering the delicate chain of the locket she never removed from her neck. This anxious question would start the tears and the choked sobs. It was then the friendship of the three counted most.

Their cots were side by side in the vast dormitory and, when any one of the three was suddenly gripped by a terrible longing for comfort, her little hand would grope between the cots to find the others' extended in silent understanding.

Their ages varied by a matter of a year, but when tested, it was found they were at the same grade level. Kit, the eldest of the trio, had already had a year of schooling and had kept up her reading skills by reading to her little brother Jamie. Laurel's mother had taught her at home and Toddy, though the youngest of the three, had learned to read from playbills and theater posters, sheet music and railroad schedules.

Separately they had suffered the most traumatic experience in life. Together they helped each other survive by reassuring themselves and each other that soon their parent would come to get them, take them away from Greystone.

After the first long week, Laurel received a letter from her mother. A note, actually. Lily had written:

My darling little girl,

This can be only a few lines. They want me to rest and don't allow me to write more than this. I am getting better every day. Soon we'll be together again. Don't forget to be a good girl and say your prayers every day, especially for your loving mother.

Enclosed was a picture postcard with the words SARANAC LAKE SANATORIUM identifying a low, rambling rustic building surrounded by pine trees with porches all along the front. Lillian had drawn a tiny arrow to one of them, printing above it,

"This is where I sit out in the sun and fresh air every day."

Laurel looked at the picture, trying to imagine her mother on the small porch. Then she put the letter and picture under her pillow. She unfolded it and read it so many times it became creased and worn around the edges.

Every week Laurel laboriously printed a letter to her mother with her version of daisies, her mother's favorite flower, drawn carefully down the border and on the flap of the envelope. Then she gave it to Miss Massey to address and mail.

Laurel never forgot the day that Miss Massey took her by the hand and led her into Miss Clinock's office.

"Sit down, Laurel, I have something to tell you," the Head Matron said. In her hands were two envelopes which Laurel immediately recognized from the daisies on them — the same daisies she always drew on her letters to Mama.

However, there was something else printed in bold black letters across the front. She could not make it out, so Miss Clinock held up the letter so Laurel could see. Slowly Laurel spelled out D-E-C-E-A-S-E-D. DECEASED.

"Do you know what this word means,

Laurel?" Miss Clinock asked kindly.

Laurel shook her head but her heart began a drumbeat that felt as if her chest were exploding. "No, ma'am," she replied in a hoarse whisper.

"It means, Laurel, that your mother is dead."

Dead! Dead? Laurel did not know what dead was! Mrs. Campbell's old cat had died, she remembered, and once she had heard Mrs. Campbell tell a visiting neighbor while pointing a thumb at Laurel, "The child's father is dead." But Mama had always told her her Papa was in Heaven with the angels. Did that mean —

Laurel could neither move nor speak. She simply sat there, glued to the straight chair opposite Miss Clinock's desk.

"Are you all right, Laurel?" prompted the Head Matron. "Do you understand what I just told you?"

Suddenly everything got very bright and hot. The room tilted crazily and the pictures on the walls swayed. Laurel saw Miss Clinock rise from behind the desk and start toward her, but her approaching figure began to blur and wobble.

A roaring started in Laurel's ears, getting louder and louder as she felt herself pitch forward, plunging into a whirling black hole. The next thing she knew she was lying down, with both Miss Clinock's and Miss Massey's worried faces leaning over her. One of them propped her up.

"Here, Laurel, sip this," Miss Massey said, holding a glass of water to her lips.

Laurel never remembered too much about the next few days. Somehow they passed in a kind of gray fog. Toddy and Kit were always nearby, but it was as if she were alone. Other people were only vague images to her, while, awake or sleeping, she seemed to see her mother's face everywhere.

She was never sure when the realization actually took hold that her mother was gone forever. Lillian would never come so that they could go home together. In fact, Laurel had no home to go to — except Greystone. She had become just like all the other children. An orphan.

When Laurel was told she was among the children from Greystone who would be traveling west on the Orphan Train, her first reaction was fear of the unknown. But as soon as she knew Kit and Toddy would be going, too, it was all right. Toddy's excitement was contagious and soon Laurel was looking forward to the day when they would meet Reverend and Mrs. Scott, representatives of the

Christian Rescuers and Providers Society, and their escorts on the trip west.

The children were given small cardboard suitcases in which to pack their few belongings to take with them on the long trip to their new lives in the Midwest.

To her dismay Laurel discovered she had outgrown all the lovely, handmade smocked and embroidered clothes her mother had made for her. So she had to accept the small wardrobe given to each girl for the journey. The garments were serviceable, if plain — a warm merino dress of dark blue, two cotton pinafores, one to wear and one to keep clean for the stops in the rural towns where the adoptions would take place, two changes of underwear, chemises, pantaloons, two petticoats, three pairs of cotton stockings, and a flannel nightgown. All the girls were issued a warm coat and bonnet and a new pair of high-top black boots with two sets of laces. All these were purchased from contributions made to the Rescuers and Providers Society by interested donors.

But as she packed, Laurel slipped into her suitcase one of the finely tucked and lace-edged camisoles her mother had made. Even if it didn't fit, it had come from beloved hands. Besides her locket, it was the only thing Laurel had left of her life before Greystone.

3

Meadowridge

On a glorious spring Sunday Dr. Leland Woodward drove his small black buggy into the cleared area between the Community Church and Ryan's pasture. He sat for a minute, the reins slack in his hands, listening to the voices floating out from inside the white frame building.

Smiling, he hummed along with them. "Blessed assurance, Jesus is mine! Oh, what a foretaste of Glory Divine —" It was one of his favorite hymns.

He knew he was late arriving for the eleven o'clock service, but he'd had to go home first to bathe, shave and change. He had been out most of the night delivering the Storms' new baby. But he didn't feel tired. In fact, he was exhilarated. Helping bring a new life into the world always gave him a boost that lasted for days. That is, if there weren't complications.

And everything had gone splendidly this time. Irma Storm was a healthy young woman who'd had no problems giving birth to a fine baby boy. Her husband Tom was a happy man. That made four sons for the Storms. Good for a farmer. In the next few years, Tom would have his own crew of harvesters come haying time! Leland chuckled. Children — that's what life was all about really. Suddenly the expression on his lean, handsome face saddened and unconsciously he sighed.

He ran his hand through his thick, prematurely gray hair, then reached for his hat on the seat beside him, put it on, gave the brim a snap, and got down from the buggy, his movements agile for a man nearing forty. Leland tethered his mare to a nearby tree, close enough to the fence so she could reach over and nibble some of the long meadow grass.

Mounting the church steps, he walked inside. One of the ushers saw him and greeted him. Leland dismissed with a gesture the offer of assistance to show him to a seat, but took the hymnal he was handed, then stood for a moment at the back looking around.

He and Ava used to have a regular pew they sat in every Sunday, but that was when

— Leland checked another sigh. Ava didn't attend church with him nowadays. Hadn't for nearly two years. Folks seemed to under-stand and yet maybe he should insist. Maybe it would help. Even seeing the chil-dren filing out for Sunday school before the sermon might jolt her from her malaise. But nothing really seemed to help.

His eyes made a quick search for an empty spot. It was better to sit near the door. That way, if anyone should need to send for him during the service, he could slip out without disturbing the congregation or start any buzzing speculation among them as to who might have taken sick or had an accident. Or been shot!

Leland suppressed a wry smile. When he had first arrived here right out of Medical School, Meadowridge was only a mere twenty years away from its roots as a raw mining town. Often he'd had to patch up the rowdies who had gotten into some Saturday night fiasco or other, and a few times some fellow got "trigger happy." Mostly ended up shooting his own foot. But that was a long time ago. Things had settled down quite a bit since then. When the women and chil-dren came, schools and churches and houses were built. Decent family folk wanted a decent town to live in, and farming became more popular and productive than searching for gold in the hills that rimmed the pretty valley.

Leland saw a seat at the end of the row in one of the last pews and moved toward it with his light, springy step. Everyone occupying that bench shifted over one to make room for him, nodding and smiling a greeting. The town's only doctor was well liked.

The last of the opening hymns sung, there was a general murmuring of voices, rustling skirts, and shuffling of Sunday-shined shoes, as the congregation settled in for one of Reverend Brewster's sermons. Leland sat back, folded his arms, ready to be instructed, inspired or exhorted. He was in a for a surprise, however, because the Reverend was even now announcing a guest speaker.

"Mr. Matthew Scott of the Christian Rescuers and Providers Society is here with a message today that I think will have special meaning for all of us. Living as we do in this beautiful, peaceful valley, surrounded by rolling hills, bordered by a river that gives us our pure water, abundant fish, refreshment and recreation, sheltered in our comfortable homes, lacking nothing in the way of food or clothing, we are apt to forget there are people in this world so unfortunate as to be without any of these necessities." Reverend Brewster paused significantly.

There was an uneasy stirring, glances exchanged among the parishioners as if wondering what their pastor had in store for them.

"I am not speaking only of grown men and women, but of innocent little children as well — abandoned, some of them left to fend for themselves on the streets of a great city — like New York or Boston. Ah, but I shall let Mr. Scott, who knows these sad stories better than I, tell you from his eyewitness experience of this deplorable situation. Mr. Scott, I turn the pulpit over to you."

A tall, thin young man stepped up to the lectern. He had tousled, rusty-brown hair, wore wire-rimmed glasses, and his scrawny neck rose out of a stiff, high collar that seemed too big for it. He looked like a timid, bookish college student. But when he began to speak, his voice was rich and full and he spoke with an earnest fervor and dramatic depth.

There was not a dry eye in the crowd when Mr. Scott had finished. There were the sounds of sniffles, throats being cleared, and noses being blown throughout the church building. Mr. Scott took off his glasses and wiped his own eyes before he made a last statement.

"I feel sure this appeal has not gone unheard in this community. I know the plight of these children I have described has touched some of you. If that is the case, perhaps you will then be led to open your homes to one or possibly two of these abandoned and orphaned children, to share your warm hearth, your affection, your good examples of Christian charity.

"The Christian Rescuers and Providers Society is dedicated to placing the right child in the right home. We do have certain requirements for the welfare of the child, and to help the adoptive family. Our main goal is to provide these poor lost children with Christian homes in which to be nurtured, trained up in the way they should go, to become God-fearing, law-abiding, self-supporting human beings. The alternative that awaits such children, it grieves me to mention, may be a life lived on the streets, forced into crime and degradation at an early age with the inevitable result — incarceration in one of our nation's prisons. Need I say more? I feel sure your generous hearts will respond. Anyone who may be interested in talking with me further, please see me after the service. I will remain as long as there are questions."

Leland swallowed hard. He had felt an increasing stricture in his throat as Scott had spoken. In spite of his outwardly impersonal professional manner, Leland Woodward had a tender heart that was easily touched, and he had been greatly moved by this talk.

He rarely showed his emotions, however. Even in the great tragedy of his life, the death of his little daughter from diphtheria at the age of seven, he had maintained a stoic composure. It was his grief-stricken wife to whom the sympathy had flowed. Perhaps feeling that a doctor was accustomed to dealing with death, people assumed he could cope with Dorie's death. Many homes had been ravaged by the terrible epidemic that had swept through Meadowridge at that time. They did not know Leland tortured himself that he might be to blame for his little girl's death. Had he somehow brought the infection home to his own child? No one could comfort him for no one knew the depth of his sorrow, his self-scourging, his guilt.

So many came to mourn with Ava. And one by one they had come away shaking their heads. "Her heart is broken. She'll never get over it."

Leland wondered if she ever would. It had

been nearly two years since they had lost their only child. Now Ava scarcely ever left the house. She never came to church, saw friends, involved herself in any of her old activities, the things she used to enjoy.

Leland knew his wife was in what was clinically called "melancholia," a depression so deep nothing seemed to be able to lift the dark cloud of sorrow from her.

She had kept Dorie's room untouched. The child's dolls, toys, playthings and books remained as though she might come running in from school at any minute.

Leland knew it was unhealthy. Everything should be put away, given away, swept out of sight. It only aggravated his wife's condition, kept her moored in the same desperate state of inconsolable sadness. But he, though a man of medicine who brought healing to others, was helpless to help the one he loved so dearly.

Leland saw the line of church members forming to meet Mr. Scott. They were clustering around him, asking questions, finding out more about the Orphan Train that would be coming west and would be making a stop in Meadowridge.

He hesitated, turning his broad-brimmed gray felt hat in his hands thoughtfully. Better not to act precipitously. Certainly, he would have to talk to Ava first.

Was it too late to reach her? He missed desperately the sound of a child's voice, laughter in the house, of running feet on the stairs. Would Ava consent, could she accept another child into her life, one who needed her?

He thought of the charming girl he had married — her laughing hazel eyes, her sparkling smile and happy nature. Was it possible she could be that way again? Maybe a child could bring it all back.

Was it worth suggesting? Worth bringing all the old wounding memories to the surface? Then he thought of the darkened room where his wife spent most of her days, staring out the window, or wandering into the bedroom with the white wicker furniture, the dollhouse and bookshelves of fairy tales that had belonged to the little girl who was gone.

It couldn't go on. Something would change. Ava would break — Leland shuddered unconsciously. No, he had to do something, take some action before it was too late. Ava could slip over the brink, and he would have lost not only his daughter but his beloved wife as well.

He would wait until just before the Orphan Train was due to come before he pressed for a decision. In the meantime he would gently persuade her to start thinking about it. Ava loved children. She was made to be a mother. Unfortunately nature had made it impossible for her to bear another child physically — but in her heart? Surely that gentle, caring heart was able to love another child.

In the meantime he would sincerely seek God's will in the matter. Leland had always asked the good Lord for guidance and direction in his life. And so far, he had never failed to get it.

4

Laurel saw her face reflected in the train window as if in a mirror. She stared out into the darkness as the Orphan Train sped across the prairie through the night.

With her finger she began to spell out her name on the gritty surface of the windowsill. "LAUREL VESTAL."

As she wrote, she formed the words silently with her tongue: "My name is Laurel Vestal." The metallic clickety-clack of the train wheels along the steel rails seemed to repeat them. *Laurel Vestal, Laurel Vestal, Laurel Vestal.*

Laurel moved, shifting her position on the hard coach seat. Her head felt hot and she leaned it against the cool glass of the window. Her throat was scratchy, too. Noticing she looked slightly feverish, Mrs. Scott had made up two of the seats into a bed earlier than usual so Laurel could lie down.

"You'll feel better in the morning," Mrs. Scott said, tucking the blanket around Laurel's shoulder. "We can't have you sick when we get to Meadowridge, now can we? Who would want to take a sick little girl home with them?"

Even though Mrs. Scott had spoken teasingly, it worried Laurel. Who, indeed, would want to take her home anyway? Because it was the first time Laurel had not been surrounded by other children for weeks, she allowed her secret fears to emerge. It was the secret fear of all the children on the Orphan Train, really, although nobody talked about it. What if nobody wanted her? No family adopted her?

Laurel closed her eyes and wished — the old wish, the one that never came true. She tried to wish herself back to the little flat on the top floor of Mrs. Campbell's house, tried to hear her mother playing on the piano, tried to recall the melodies of her favorite pieces — "Annie Laurie" or "The Robin's Return" — feel that warm, sweet security of her mother's presence again.

She sighed, a sigh that came from deep inside. If only she had Miranda to cuddle. Why hadn't she remembered to carry her doll with her that last morning when she and her mother had left the apartment?

Laurel blinked, trying not to cry. Her mother had said there would be lots of toys to play with where she was going. But at Greystone the toys had to be shared with everyone, and there were never enough to go around. Besides, none of the dolls could replace her beautiful Miranda. Most of them were worn, battered, the wigs gone, the paint chipped off their faces.

Unconsciously Laurel's hand moved to her neck, fingering the chain and locket that held her mother's and father's pictures. She had promised Mama she would never take it off. At least "until I come to get you." Recalling her mother's words, Laurel felt angry.

Why had her mother not told her the truth? About Greystone? About how sick she was and that she might die? Now, Laurel could not halt the tears. They rolled down one by one and, as she brushed them away, they made sooty streaks on her cheeks.

What had become of all their things? Her books, her doll's bed, the little china tea set that had belonged to Mama herself when *she* was a little girl? The piano and the painting her father had done that hung over it, the one of the lighthouse at Cape Cod? When

41

they hadn't come back, had Mrs. Campbell taken everything up to her attic?

Once Laurel had gone there with Mrs. Campbell when she had lugged up some big boxes that some tenant had left behind. Laurel remembered Mrs. Campbell saying, "You just never know when a person may show up again. And as long as I've got the room, why not? Poor Mr. Lonergan might have had a spell of bad luck, or been hit over the head and lost his memory or something, who can tell?"

Mrs. Campbell was an avid reader of the kind of newspaper that printed the dramatic catastrophes of life in lurid detail. Laurel had a vivid picture of the woman, sitting in her kitchen rocker with the newspaper spread open, clucking her tongue and shaking her head as she read out loud some of the headlines of the stories printed on its pages: "Excursion Boat Capsizes, All on Board Perish," or "Fire Ravages Building, Frenzied Tenants Leap to Their Death."

Mrs. Campbell had probably packed all their belongings neatly and carried them up to her attic. That thought gave Laurel a little comfort.

Just then the mournful sound of the train whistle hooted shrilly as they approached a crossing. Laurel huddled further into the skimpy blanket and pressed her face against the window, peering out eagerly. Laurel liked it when the train slowed a little going through a small town and she could see lights like little yellow squares in the houses they passed. They looked so inviting, so cozy. She tried to imagine who lived there, what kind of family, how many children, what they were doing. Maybe a mother knitting, a father smoking a pipe, children playing on the floor, maybe a baby in a cradle nearby. She would try to imagine what it would be like to be inside — safe, happy, secure.

The familiar longing gripped her heart, bringing on that uncomfortable, choking sensation, a kind of emptiness, that started in the pit of her stomach and spread slowly through the rest of her.

Behind her, Laurel could hear the other children's voices as they finished up a game they were playing. Above all the others, Toddy's voice taking the lead, giving orders. She was glad Toddy was her friend, and Kit. It was Toddy who had come up with the plan of how the three of them could stay together, be adopted in the same town at least. At first, Laurel thought her idea was wrong, like telling lies. But then Toddy had explained it was just like being in a play! And it was the only way they could be *sure* they wouldn't be separated. Of course, Mrs. Scott had scolded them when she discovered what Toddy had coached them to do — Kit, dragging her leg as if she were crippled; Toddy, crossing her eyes and twisting her face into the most awful grimace, and Laurel, hunching one shoulder higher than the other as she walked.

Even though they had gotten into trouble for doing it, Laurel was glad it had worked. There was only one more stop on the trip. Meadowridge. Here they would all find homes. Here, in the same town where they could go to school together and see each other often. That was important. Without Toddy and Kit, Laurel didn't know what she would do.

Unconsciously, Laurel shuddered. She dreaded having all those grown-ups staring at her at every train stop. Trying *not* to get adopted had been bad, but now that she wanted to be adopted, it was even scarier.

The day after tomorrow, they would be in Meadowridge. Mrs. Scott had shown them where it was on the map she had pinned up on the wall. She said it was about the pleasantest town she had ever seen, that she would like to live there herself instead of in

Pennsylvania where she and Mr. Scott lived.

Laurel's eyes began to feel heavy. She was sleepy. She pushed the lumpy pillow under her head and closed her eyes. No matter what, even if it *was* scary, it was better being on the Orphan Train on its way to Meadowridge and being adopted — than staying at Greystone and being an *orphan!*

5

"Just to make sure no one's coming down with some contagious disease with which a whole family could be infected," Dr. Woodward had volunteered to give each of the Orphan Train children a brief physical checkup before he or she was "placed out" in one of the adoptive homes. Reverend Brewster, on the advice of Mr. Scott, had suggested it might be a good idea.

On the morning of the Orphan Train's arrival, Leland stopped at the door of his wife's darkened sitting room, and stood there for a moment frowning. Then, striving to sound cheerful, he spoke. "It's a beautiful day, my dear. Why do you have the shutters closed and the curtains drawn? Let me open them, let in some of that lovely sunshine," he urged and started to move toward the windows.

"No, please, Lee," she protested, raising a fragile hand. "I have a slight headache. The glare bothers my eyes."

Leland halted then went over to the chaise lounge where Ava Woodward lay. He lifted her thin wrist in his fingers, automatically feeling for her pulse. He placed his other hand on her forehead but it felt cool to his touch.

"Do you think you'll feel better later? Well enough to accompany me to the train station? The Orphan Train is due in at one o'clock."

"Oh, no, Lee, I couldn't." Ava shook her head.

"But the child — don't you want to help me choose?" he persisted gently.

"No —" she murmured. "It was your decision —"

Leland checked a quick spurt of irritation. "But we discussed it thoroughly, my dear, and you agreed."

"Because you wanted it so, Leland." Ava sighed deeply. "You can be very persuasive."

Leland felt his fists clench. "Ava, if you had any doubts about this, you should have expressed them when I first brought up the subject, not wait until *now* . . . the very day the children are coming."

Her fingers picked at the fringe of the shawl wrapped around her frail shoulders.

She did not meet his pleading eyes.

"I've had the room made ready," she said meekly.

But your heart, is it ready? Leland asked mentally, gazing down at his wife.

She raised her head and, seeing his beseeching look, reached for his hand. "Be patient with me, Lee. It will take time —"

"It's been two years, my dear. It's time we got on with our lives." He paused. "A child is what this house needs now. You said so yourself—"

"I know, Lee. I thought I was ready. But, now, I don't know —" her voice wavered uncertainly.

Leland tried to control his impatience. He took out his watch and consulted it.

"I have to make house calls. I'll be back by noon. Please, dear, make the effort to come with me to the train. It would mean a great deal to me. And to the child."

He leaned down and kissed her on her cheek, then left the room and the house in an agony of indecision. Maybe it had been a mistake to talk Ava into taking one of the Orphan Train children. Perhaps a terrible mistake.

But down deep, Leland didn't think so. He felt it was the right thing. At any rate he was committed now. He had written the

Rescuers and Providers Society that he and his wife would take a child into their home. He had stipulated a boy. A boy, he felt, would be easier for Ava than a little girl. It would be too hard for her to accept another little girl . . . after Dorie.

Like most men, Leland Woodward had always wanted a son. Dreamed of having one. A lad everyone would call "Doc's boy," to ride along in the buggy with him when he made house calls. He planned to get him interested early in science, buy him a microscope, send him to one of the best medical colleges, and then when he got his degree, he could go into practice with his father.

Leland had adored his little daughter, but still had longed for a son. When it was definite Ava and he would never have another child of their own, Leland had put away his dreams of a son to follow in his footsteps. But now that possibility had arisen once more. An adopted boy he could bring up as he would have his own son. It could all still happen.

In spite of Ava's resistance, Leland felt fairly sure that once the boy was in their home, she would come around. Yes, Leland reassured himself, he had made the right decision.

At twenty minutes before one o'clock,

Leland arrived at the Meadowridge Church Social Hall — alone. When he had returned home after making house calls, Ava was still lying on the chaise, now with a cologne-dampened cloth over her eyes. She felt too indisposed to go with him, she whispered. Knowing it was useless, he had not argued.

But while he arranged his makeshift office, adjusting the window blind for more light, filling a glass tumbler with wooden tongue depressors, Leland's mind was troubled. Suppose Ava really did not want a child. Evidently she had made herself ill over the prospect. What should he do now? He supposed another home could be found for the boy. He had not signed anything legal; he could explain to the Scotts —

Leland had no more time to consider the problem because the door of the Social Hall opened and there was a rush of voices as a crowd of people entered. Soon he was busy peering down little throats, checking ears, listening to the thrumming of dozens of healthy little hearts.

As one child after the other filed into this temporary medical facility, Leland felt that old yearning for a child grow stronger. Each child whose clear eyes he looked into, each pink tongue he depressed, each pair of lungs he pronounced sound intensified his desire to take one home with him.

Leland had always had a wonderful way with children. He could calm their fears with affectionate teasing, dry their tears with a fond tweaking of a nose, always holding out the jar of hard candies he kept alongside for a small hand to dip into when the examination was over.

"Next!" he called out to one of the church ladies who was standing in the doorway ushering in the next small "patient."

Leland finished the paperwork on the last patient before he looked up to greet the newcomer. When he did so, he stared right into the eyes of the prettiest little girl he had seen that day. At the same time it was with a stab of recognition. It was uncanny. This child could have been Ava at the same age!

Tendrils of dark hair curled around a rosy face and fell in lustrous curls onto her shoulders. Long-lashed brown eyes regarded him steadily, a tiny tentative, smile tugging at the rosebud mouth.

Leland held out both hands. "Well, little lady, come in. Don't be afraid. I won't hurt you. What is your name?" he asked.

"Laurel," she replied, approaching him slowly. She didn't seem afraid but had a sort of touching dignity.

Poor little tyke, Leland thought. A long

journey, now this.

He proceeded with the examination, allowing Laurel to hold the tongue depressor before he looked down her throat, let her listen to *his* chest, hear *his* heart beat, then place the stethoscope on her own while he listened.

All the while he spoke to her gently, all thoughts of the boy he had planned to take home with him slowly vanishing from Leland's mind. If God had blessed him and Ava with another little girl of their own, she couldn't have looked more like this child. The longer he talked to her, the more he gazed into her sweet little face, saw her smile, heard her laugh at his silly jokes, the more convinced Leland became that this was the child he was meant to have. And the conviction grew within him that this child would bring with her the blessing he had prayed for, to his wife, to their marriage, to their home. With her, God would restore the joy that had been missing so long.

Had he not asked God for direction? This strong inner drawing toward this little girl *must* be His sign. How else was he to know God's will but in the very human feelings he was experiencing?

He leaned forward and took both Laurel's little hands in his.

"Would you like to come home with me,

Laurel, be my little girl? We have a big back yard with trees and a swing. And there's even a pond with goldfish swimming in it. I think you would like it."

Laurel looked into the strong face searching hers for an answer. Behind his glasses, kindly blue eyes twinkled. She felt the warmth reach out from him to enfold her.

"Well, Laurel, what do you say?"

"Yes." She nodded solemnly.

Leland felt his heart leap. Suddenly his glasses misted and he took out his handkerchief to wipe them. Then, clearing his throat, he said, "Come on, then, let's make it official."

Leland made short work of the red tape. Having completed all the necessary papers with his usual dispatch, he was getting ready to leave when he saw the Hansens.

He hesitated for a minute, wondering whether to speak to them or not. Although their farm was a good distance from Meadowridge Township, he had delivered all five of their children. The last two had been difficult births for Mrs. Hansen, a case of too many, too close together and not much time to recover before the next pregnancy. He'd warned her to be careful, to let up on some of the heavier chores for a while.

53

"Those big fellows of yours are old enough and strong enough to take on some of the load, aren't they?" he had asked her.

She had nodded meekly, but said nothing. Her husband had been present. Maybe that was it. Was Cora Hansen afraid of her husband?

Dr. Woodward turned away without greeting them. He didn't much like Jess Hansen. Seemed an insensitive, uncaring sort.

Just then Reverend Brewster spoke and Leland turned to answer him. When he looked again, he saw Jess Hansen with a little girl following him. At the door she turned to wave at Laurel, who waved back.

Leland lifted Laurel up into the buggy, placing the small suitcase on the floor in front of her so she could put her feet on it. Then he went around, got in beside her, smiled down at her as he picked up the reins.

"Well, Laurel, we're off. We're going home."

Home! The word made Laurel feel strange, excited but at the same time a little afraid. She had not allowed herself to think "home" or say the word for months. Home meant the cozy, little rooms on the top of Mrs. Campbell's house. She had missed it so much, and Mama — Laurel felt the old sadness sweep over her and she resolutely set her jaw and looked out around her.

Dr. Leland's horse trotted along a pleasant, curving street lined with shade trees. Neat houses were set back from the road, with pretty gardens behind picket fences. Then they slowed to a halt, and the horse stopped in front of a white frame house without Dr. Woodward even saying "Whoa!"

Laurel glanced at it curiously. It had lace curtains at the dark green shuttered windows, and baskets of pink geraniums swung along the railings at the top of the deep porch. It looked like a nice house, a friendly house, Laurel thought as Dr. Woodward helped her down, took her hand and led her up the steps and into the house.

"Are you hungry, Laurel? Would you like something to eat?" he asked.

Laurel shook her head and said politely, "No, thank you."

Thinking she might be refusing out of shyness, Leland suggested, "Well, I am, and thirsty, too. I'll tell you what. We'll go into the kitchen and see if Ella, our cook, has some lemonade and maybe some cookies. Then we'll go upstairs so you can meet my wife. Come on," he said, and Leland took

Laurel's hand again and led her into the sunny spotless kitchen.

A half hour later, Ella Mason, the cook, hands on her hips, raised her eyebrows and looked at Jenny Appleton, the hired girl who came three days a week to clean.

"Well, what do you think of this?"

It was more a declaration than a question, so Jenny shrugged.

"What the missus will say is what I'm wonderin'." Ella gave a shake of her head.

"Well —" Jenny ventured, but Ella went on as if talking to herself and did not notice.

Ella got out the vegetables she was preparing to scrub and shook one of the carrots to emphasize her words. "She'd agreed to a boy, you know."

"Girls aren't so messy or noisy either, for that matter," Jenny declared, thinking of her own mother's brood of six and the bedlam Jen went home to each evening.

Ella rolled out dough for a pie on the cutting board.

"She's never got over it, you see. The little girl dyin' like that." Ella shook her head. "Don't know as if she can take to another one. It would be like she was trying to replace Dorie, don't you know?"

Jenny leaned against the counter listening. She had only worked for the

56

Woodwards this past year. But of course the whole town knew about their tragedy.

"I say, either way, it's a good thing," Ella went on. "This house has been gloomy too long. A child will make a difference, boy *or* girl."

"That's for sure." Jenny nodded. "When I first come here to work, it was so quiet it near gave me the creeps. I used to say to Ma when I'd go home in the evenin' that I didn't even mind the noise there so much after being here all day. I told her —"

But Ella wasn't interested in whatever Jenny had told her mother. A seraphic expression suddenly crossed her plump, rosy-cheeked face. "I think I'll make a custard pudding for tonight. Children like something smooth and sweet, you know." She paused, then remarked thoughtfully, "She's a pretty little thing, ain't she?"

Ella opened a cabinet, took out a big bowl, got down the basket of fresh eggs, and began cracking them one by one into it.

Jen realized the discussion was over for now. Ella was too busy with her recipe to talk.

Jenny went to the broom closet and got out the carpet sweeper. She'd just do the rugs in the hall downstairs and see if she could hear anything to report back to Ella when the doctor took the little Orphan Train girl upstairs to meet the mistress.

Jenny felt sorry for Mrs. Woodward, although she did not know her very well. She was a pretty, dark-haired lady, even if she was too thin and had such mournful eyes. She spoke in a soft voice and gave very few directions about the housework Jenny was to do, but spent most of her time in her upstairs sitting room.

One afternoon Jenny had ventured up with a note from Dr. Woodward, delivered by a hospital messenger. The note said he had an emergency and would be late coming home for dinner. The note could have gone straight to Ella, Jen found out. In fact, after she'd read it, Mrs. Woodward had folded it and asked Jenny to take it down to the kitchen.

But it was *where* Jenny had found Mrs. Woodward that had been so strange and sad. She had knocked at the sitting room door which was always closed. When there was no answer, Jenny had inched it slowly open. But Mrs. Woodward wasn't in there.

Thinking she might have one of her sick headaches — and might be lying down, Jenny tiptoed down the hall to the bedroom. But the door was ajar and she was not in there either.

Then Jenny had heard the sound of sobbing. It came from directly across the hall. Turning, Jenny could see through the half-open door leading into a spacious, airy room flooded with sunlight. It was a room that she had never been asked to clean or dust, a child's room, belonging to a little girl, from the looks of it. And there sitting on the floor by the window seat was Mrs. Woodward, in front of a big dollhouse, holding a teddy bear in her lap.

Jenny stood there frozen, the note in her hand, not knowing whether to go or stay. Just then Mrs. Woodward had turned her head and seen her. For a few seconds neither of them moved nor spoke. Then Mrs. Woodward got to her feet and came over to the door. "What is it, Jenny?" she asked quietly.

Jenny could see that her pale cheeks were wet with tears. Embarrassed, she had stuttered out about the boy from the hospital and handed Mrs. Woodward the note.

Later, back in the kitchen, Jenny related what she had seen to Ella.

"Oh, my, don't I know?" Ella clucked her tongue. "She didn't want a thing in that room touched after Dorie died. With my own ears, I've heard the doctor beg her many times, 'Ava, please,' he'd say, 'you're

59

just making it harder on yourself,' and she'd say, so pitiful, 'Lee, I can't, it would be like losing her forever. It's all I have left.' "

Remembering that incident and the conversation with Ella afterwards, Jenny unconsciously shook her head. Would this Orphan Train girl *really* make a difference? Or would it just make things worse?

Leland left Laurel sitting on the porch swing when he went upstairs to tell Ava what he had done. He found her still lying on her chaise in her sitting room. He told her as quietly and quickly as he could.

Ava Woodward stared at her husband with an expression of grieved betrayal.

"Oh, Lee, how could you? Bringing a little girl into this house . . . she could never take Dorie's place!"

"She's not intended to take Dorie's place. No one could do that. She'll make her own place here. Give her time. Give yourself time, a chance to know her," he entreated.

Ava shook her head, tears glistening in her dark eyes as she looked at him in disbelief.

"You said you were getting a boy and I agreed to that. I understood what a boy would mean to you." She clasped her thin hands together, held them to her chin in a pleading gesture. "You know how I longed to give you a son of your own." Ava closed her eyes, recalling the months, the years, her hopes had risen only to be dashed. "But this . . . you're asking too much of me, Leland?"

"Darling, I would never knowingly do anything to hurt you." He took a step toward her, but she held up her hand to ward him off, turning her head away from him as he leaned forward to kiss her.

The silence that followed stretched interminably between them. She did not move to stop him as he went to the door, stood there for a full minute. Then she heard the door close quietly behind him as he left the room.

6

The few days after Laurel arrived at the Woodwards had been the longest Ava could remember. After her first startled reaction to the fact that, instead of a boy orphan of about ten or twelve, Leland had brought home a little girl nearly the same age as the child they had lost, Ava had maintained a cold, hurt silence.

It seemed an unspeakable breach of understanding on his part, an inexplicable lack of empathy for Leland who was usually so considerate, so kind. It had created a chasm between them, wider and more dangerous than any difficulty or difference they had ever faced in their fifteen-year marriage.

Ava had not come downstairs for breakfast since Dorie died because she could not sleep at night unless she took the sleeping draughts Leland meted out to her sparingly.

Since Laurel's coming, she stayed in bed until she heard Leland leave the house to go on his house calls every morning. Then Ava shut herself up in her sitting room. She refused to allow herself to wonder what the little girl did with herself. It was, after all, Lee's responsibility, she told herself, and she assumed he had made arrangements for Jenny to look out for the child.

She and Leland had had the worst argument of their entire marriage the night he had brought the little girl here. They had both said things they knew they would regret later. But the hurtful words had been said and still hung between them tensely.

Leland had slept on the couch in his office, as he often did when Ava was unwell, and had been uncomfortably sleepless and troubled. He spent a good deal of the night praying that Ava would relent, would come around and accept Laurel, who had to be the dearest little girl in the world.

The third morning, Ava rose and stood at her door, listening to Leland speaking to someone downstairs. The child? Hearing the front door close, Ava lifted shaking hands to her throbbing temples. She had awakened with all the frightful warning signals. She knew the signs — the shooting flashes of light zigzagging before her eyes, the dizziness, the tension in her stomach, the clamminess of her palms — all signaling the onset of a sick headache.

She should have known! Getting so upset always brought on one of her migraines.

She pressed her fingers over her eyes for a minute. Dear God, what was she to do? She dearly loved her husband, had always tried to comply with his wishes. And she wanted him to be happy, wanted to live up to his expectations of her, but *this* she simply could not do!

Ava had prayed about accepting a boy. At length, she had seemed to have peace about it, even though she knew it would be difficult, at least at first. But a boy was so different in every way from a girl that there would have been no reminders of her own little daughter. A girl nearly the same age as Dorie would have been if she had lived? Well, that was simply too much to ask of her!

Ava walked over to the window overlooking the garden. Pushing the curtain aside, she looked down and saw Leland, hand in hand with the little girl, walking along the flagstone path to the back gate leading out to the stable.

Leland was going on his house calls this time of day, Ava knew. She watched as Leland bent down, one hand gently stroking the child's long, dark curls as he talked to her. Then he kissed her cheek and went through the gate. The little girl jumped on the bottom ledge, leaning over the top and waving her hand. For a few minutes the child stayed there, swinging back and forth on the open gate. Then as the sounds of Leland's horse's hoofs and buggy wheels died away, she got down, turned and started walking back through the garden.

There was something pathetic about the droop of her shoulders, the way her feet lagged, an air of loneliness about the small figure in the drab denim dress and pinafore. In spite of herself, Ava's heart was touched.

Suddenly the stabbing pain in her head made Ava sway slightly. She grabbed onto the nearby chair to steady herself, then staggering with vertigo, she stumbled over to her chaise lounge and lowered herself onto it.

If she could only sleep for a few hours, the headache might go away or at least diminish. She prayed for oblivion, to block out not only the physical pain, but the pain of her heart's distress. She prayed to be released from her feeling of guilt and failure. She prayed to be free of the sting of Leland's accusation that she was shutting out a child who needed caring parents, a home.

★ ★ ★

Laurel sat on the bottom step of the polished staircase. The house was hushed. There was not a sound anywhere. Not the rattle of pans or the noise of any activity coming from the kitchen, for this was Ella's afternoon off. No murmur of voices or of doors opening and closing, people coming and going from the doctor's office at the side of the house. Dr. Woodward kept office hours only three mornings a week. The other days he went to see sick people in their homes. Today he would be gone all afternoon, he had told Laurel when he left.

Laurel sighed. She was lonely. She was glad to be in this lovely big house with Dr. Woodward. But she missed her two friends, Kit and Toddy. Dr. Woodward had promised she could have them over to play in a few weeks.

That was a long time to wait. Laurel sighed again. But Dr. Woodward said his wife had not been well and until she felt better it would be best not to have other children here.

Laurel had only seen Mrs. Woodward briefly. She was a very pretty lady, but when Dr. Woodward took Laurel in to meet her that first evening, she looked very pale and had only murmured a few words. Then Dr. Woodward sent Laurel out to the hall, telling her to wait for him there. She had stood uncertainly just outside the sitting room door, not knowing what else to do. And that was when she heard Mrs. Woodward say, "Lee, why in the world did you bring that child here?"

Remembering, a sad little ache pressed against Laurel's chest. Mrs. Woodward did not want her. So what was going to happen to her? Would she be "placed out" somewhere else? Just thinking about it gave her that scary feeling again.

But Dr. Woodward was so nice. He seemed to like having her here, and everyone else was so kind. Ella, the cook, was jolly and Jenny, who came three times a week, was always friendly and ready to chat.

But today Jenny hadn't come and the house seemed big and empty. What could she do all afternoon? Laurel wondered. There was nothing much for a girl to play with here. Funny, but the room Dr. Woodward had said was hers that first night held lots of things a *boy* might like! There were books about Indians, a building game, and a set of toy soldiers. But Laurel would have liked something like paper dolls to cut out, or jackstraws or a book of fairy tales.

She sighed again and took out her locket, pressed the place on the back that snapped it open, and looked long and lovingly at the pictures in the two ovals. Laurel still missed her mother. But their life together at Mrs. Campbell's was getting dimmer and dimmer. Of course, she didn't want to forget, but there had been so many new experiences since then. Still, she always looked at the pictures and kissed the photos of her parents every night before going to bed.

Sometimes she lay in bed, reliving some of the things she and Mama used to do together. Certain things they did every week, like taking the rent money down to Mrs. Campbell.

Laurel remembered how Mama would carefully count out the exact amount, taking it from the tin box where she put the money her students paid for their music lessons and placing it in the envelope marked RENT. There were other envelopes marked FOOD, TITHE, CLOTHING MATERIAL, even one marked FUN. That was the one Laurel liked best, because out of that came the rare cups of ice cream they bought at the stand in the park after a trip to the Zoo, or a new piece of music for Mama to learn, then teach to her piano students. Sometimes

FUN meant an excursion downtown. Taking a horse-car was always an adventure, and then those special trips to the Art Museum. There, Mama would show her the big paintings in gold frames that hung in room after room in a vast building.

"Your father was an artist, Laurel," Mama would say, her eyes very bright.

"Did he paint these?" Laurel once asked, pointing.

"No, he had to sell most of his work. Although some of the ones I thought were his best ones didn't sell. If he had lived, I believe he would have been famous," her mother told her, then added, "but I've kept them all packed away except for that one we have over the piano."

Laurel thought of that painting now. It was of a lighthouse on a cliff overlooking the ocean. The sun in the picture was very strong, casting sharp shadows on the white building and on the beach below and the sparkling blue water. It was a happy painting, one that made Laurel feel good inside when she looked at it.

"That was painted the summer we spent at Truro," Mama had told her. "You were hardly more than a baby, Laurel, but I used to take you down to the beach with me and take off your little shoes and stockings and let you put your feet in the sand. We'd sit under a big umbrella and sometimes your father would sketch us, or set up his portable easel and paint. Oh, darling, I wish you could remember!" Mama would say, looking sad.

Now, as she thought of those times, Laurel's feeling of aloneness sharpened along with an intense longing for her mother. Laurel crossed her arms and hugged herself, rocking back and forth slightly.

Time hung motionless. It would be ages before Dr. Woodward returned. Aimlessly, Laurel began to count the rungs of the stair railings on each step. Humming a little tune she recalled her mother's music students practicing over and over, she moved up slowly from step to step.

Finally, she reached the top of the stairway. Now what could she do to pass the time until Dr. Woodward came home and took her for a buggy ride as he had promised?

Laurel pulled herself to her feet, holding onto the banister. Feeling the satiny surface, she was strongly tempted to mount it and slide backwards down its smooth length. She fought the temptation for a full moment. Resisting it, she decided to go and look over the books in her room once more to see if any of them had interesting pictures. If so, she could take one outside and sit in the porch swing and look at them while she waited for Dr. Woodward to come home.

She started down the hallway toward her room when, passing a half-opened door, she halted. She had passed this room a dozen or more times before, but the door had always been closed. Now it stood open so Laurel could look inside.

Curious, Laurel moved closer and peered in. Nobody was there but it had a waiting look, as though expecting someone to come at any minute. A little girl? For surely this room was intended for a little girl, Laurel thought, inching closer.

Sun poured in through crisp, white ruffled curtains onto the flowered chintz cushions of the window seat, gilding the blond curls of a big doll seated in a small wicker chair by a low table all set with little dishes. Under the window were shelves full of toys, games, and books.

Drawn irresistibly forward, Laurel pushed open the door and stepped inside, looking around her with wide-eyed wonder.

Walking very slowly, as if in a dream, Laurel went to the middle of the room and pivoted, gazing from the scrolled white iron bed, with its ruffled coverlet, piled high with dolls and stuffed animals, to a tiny red rocking chair decorated with painted flowers in one corner next to a large, peaked-roofed dollhouse.

What a wonderful, wonderful room!

Laurel tiptoed over to the dollhouse and knelt down in front of it, gazing into the tiny rooms. There was a parlor, a bedroom, a little nursery with a canopied bassinet in which a tiny china doll nestled. There was even a kitchen, with wee little pots and pans! Laurel put out her hand to move one of the dollhouse occupants that had fallen out of a winged chair next to the fireplace, complete with brass andirons.

But just as she did, a voice from behind her ordered sharply, "Don't touch that!"

Startled, Laurel jerked around, dropping the little figure. Mrs. Woodward was standing in the doorway. Masses of dark hair tumbled wildly around her shoulders and her eyes were fiery coals.

"What are you doing in here?" she demanded furiously.

Laurel was so frightened she burst into tears.

A lavender dusk had fallen over the garden as Leland came through the gate, went up the back porch steps and into the house. There were no lamps lighted yet and Dr. Woodward set down his medical bag and stood for a few minutes, sorting through the mail left on the hall table.

Then he lifted his head in a listening attitude. From somewhere in the house, he heard the sound of soft singing — a familiar, low, sweet melody that struck a reminiscent chord deep within him. He had not heard it in a very long time. And where and when, he could not think.

He went to the bottom of the staircase and, out of long habit, started to call up that he was home. Then he thought better of it, and instead, climbed the stairway, hoping against hope that Ava might be feeling better. Their problem weighed heavily upon him. Nothing was worth this estrangement. The little girl would have to go. He must find a good home for her, a place where she would be welcomed, where she would be loved as she deserved to be loved.

When he reached the landing the sound of singing became clearer. Puzzled, he moved along the hall toward his wife's sitting room.

At the door he paused. What he saw made his heart leap. Stunned, he stood there unmoving.

The room was in shadows. Only a soft,

violet light filtering through the filmy curtains illuminated Ava's profile. She was seated in her rocker, holding Laurel in her lap, gently rocking her. The child's head rested on Ava's shoulder as if it belonged there.

When Ava saw Leland's figure silhouetted in the doorframe, she put her index finger to her smiling lips warningly.

It was then he remembered the song Ava was singing. It was the lullabye with which she used to rock Dorie to sleep.

Later that night, as Leland cradled his wife in his arms, long after they had both put Laurel to bed, she wept quietly. "Oh, Lee, to think I frightened that dear little thing, scared her into tears! I'm so ashamed. I have been so selfish, Lee, so self-absorbed, so wrapped up in my own feelings I haven't thought of anyone else's. Can you ever forgive me?"

"There's nothing to forgive, my darling," he murmured, smoothing back her hair from her forehead, tangling his fingers in its silky waves. "I love you and all I ever wanted was your happiness."

"We *will* be happy again, Lee. I feel it, I know it! And I promise you this will be a home for Laurel to be happy in, too!"

7

The Fourth of July in Meadowridge was celebrated with enthusiastic fervor — parades, picnics, political speeches, patriotic pantomimes held at the town park, with a lavish fireworks display after dark.

The whole community entered into the festive occasion. Main Street was decorated with red, white and blue bunting banners, and each storefront displayed its own American flag. At Tanner's Field, where a softball game between the town's two rival teams would be played in the afternoon, the bleachers were festooned with streamers and balloons.

By eleven o'clock families carrying wicker baskets, laden with special holiday food, began to arrive at the city park looking for the ideal spot to picnic. In the white-latticed gazebo in the center, the Meadowridge

Town Band, attired in their gold-braided, bright red jackets buttoned in shiny brass, were tuning up their instruments for the music they would be providing throughout the day.

Ava brushed Laurel's dark curls and then tied them with a dark blue satin ribbon in a flat bow.

"There now, turn around so I can see how you look."

Obediently Laurel swung away from the mirror, holding out her skirt for Ava's approval. She was wearing a blue and white striped chambray dress with a square white eyelet lace collar threaded with narrow red ribbon.

"Just perfect," Ava declared with satisfaction. "Perfect for the Fourth of July and for this beautiful summer day." She patted Laurel's cheek. "You'll be the prettiest little girl at the picnic."

"All ready to go?" asked Dr. Woodward, coming to the door of Laurel's bedroom. He looked at them both admiringly. "What a lucky man I am to be escorting two such lovely ladies."

"You *could* be slightly prejudiced, you know, Lee," Ava chided him playfully. "But isn't Laurel a picture?"

"I see two pictures," declared Dr. Woodward, beaming. "If there were going to be a beauty contest today, you would both win hands down."

"Will there be a contest?" asked Laurel.

Dr. Woodward chuckled. "Well, maybe not for beauty, but there'll be plenty of contests — potato sack races, best pie contests, watermelon eating contests — more contests than you can shake a stick at!"

Laurel giggled. Dr. Lee, as she had begun to call him, was always saying funny things like that. Who would shake a stick at a contest?

"Come on, let's get going," he urged. "You can already hear the band music from the park. We don't want to miss anything."

"Just wait until I put on my hat," Ava pleaded gaily, thrusting a long, pearl-headed pin into the band of white roses circling the crown of her straw hat. "There, we're ready!" she said with satisfaction, giving Laurel's hair ribbon a final flip.

Leland held out his arm to his wife, reached his other hand to Laurel, and the three of them went downstairs and out to the buggy. Laurel loved riding in the buggy, especially when all three of them rode together. That wasn't often because Dr. Lee needed it most of the time for his work. Today he had fastened the canvas top back so that she could feel the sun on her head and back as they trotted down the street on the way to the park.

Looking up she saw Dr. Lee, smiling over her head at Mrs. Woodward who smiled back at him. That gave Laurel a nice warm feeling in her tummy. Things at the Woodwards' had become very pleasant. The three of them spent many happy hours together. Ever since that awful time Mrs. Woodward had frightened her in Dorie's room, things had changed.

Dr. Lee had explained to Laurel about Dorie so that she understood.

"You see, Laurel, we lost our little girl just as you lost your parents. And now, we can all help each other. You'll be our little girl and we'll be your parents."

Laurel had nodded. But, unconsciously, she felt for the heart-shaped locket under her dress, as if to remind herself that no one could *ever* take the place of her *real* parents.

Dr. Woodward maneuvered his buggy between the other vehicles, buggies, wagons and gigs that were lined in zigzag rows, horses hitched to the rail fence that surrounded the park. Then he assisted Ava out, lifted Laurel down, and removed the covered picnic basket Ella had packed for them.

"Where would you like to settle, my

dear?" he asked Ava. "I see there are still some empty tables near that cluster of oak trees."

Before she had a chance to answer him, a shrill voice called, "Ava! Ava Woodward, wait a minute!"

They all turned in time to see a plump, blonde woman, holding onto her hat with one hand, while with the other she was pulling along a tousle-headed boy. Laurel recognized him as the same obnoxious boy in her Sunday school class who thought it funny to pull her curls when he stood behind her.

When she reached them, the woman said breathlessly, "Oh, Ava, my dear, it is *so* good to see you!"

Laurel felt Ava stiffen as if to ward off an unwelcome embrace. The other woman ignored this rebuff and went right on talking. "We have *all* missed *you* so. I cannot *begin* to tell you how my heart has gone out to you all these months in your sorrow. We thought, at least . . . *some people* thought you would *never* get over it and —"

"Thank you, Bernice, I appreciate that. I'd like you to meet our Laurel," she said, interrupting the sticky flow of words. "Laurel, this is Mrs. Blanchard and her son, Christopher."

At this, Mrs. Blanchard lowered her voice significantly as though Laurel were deaf and said, "When I heard you and Dr .Woodward were taking in one of those waifs, Ava, I couldn't believe it! After all you've been through to take such a chance — Why, you can't tell what kind of background they come from. I've heard most of them have lived by their wits on city streets —"

"I think you're mistaken, Bernice," Ava cut in coldly. "If you'll excuse us, Doctor is beckoning us. We must go and get our table —" Ava took Laurel's hand tightly in hers and left the woman standing there with her mouth open.

Later, Laurel overheard Ava repeating the conversation to Dr. Woodward. This time her icily polite tone of voice changed. She was obviously very angry.

Dr. Woodward tried to calm her down. "Bernice Blanchard!" he scoffed. "Everyone knows what a rattle-brain she is, speaks before she thinks, likes to hear herself talk. Don't give it another thought, my dear."

"But if she'd say a thing like that to my face, what is she saying behind my back?" demanded Ava.

"What difference does it make, darling? We know the truth. Don't let it spoil things for you."

"I just don't want her spiteful remarks to make things difficult for Laurel as she's growing up in this town. Or for any of the other Orphan Train children," Ava said.

"Put it out of your mind. It isn't that important."

"I don't know, Lee. After all, Bernice is the town banker's wife. She has a lot of influence." Ava sounded doubtful.

"It's too nice a day to worry about something like that. Remember, 'This is the day the Lord hath made, let us rejoice and be glad in it'!" the doctor said, patting his wife's hand reassuringly.

Dr. Lee often quoted the Bible, Laurel had begun to notice.

Sometimes it was his way of ending a discussion, she realized, but it was a nice way. Otherwise, Mrs. Woodward went on and on, fretting about something.

But on this lovely summer day there did not seem to be anything that could disturb anyone for long. There was not a single cloud in the sky. The sun was warm, but there was a breeze gently fanning the leaves overhead. It was, as Dr. Lee kept saying, "a grand and glorious Fourth."

Ava seated herself comfortably at a picnic table, her parasol protecting her from the sun. Lee stood, surveying the holiday activi-

81

ties underway, nodding and returning the greetings of many who passed on their way to their own picnic spots. Of course, as the town doctor, Lee was known by nearly everybody in Meadowridge. Ava was aware of a few curious looks and unconsciously put a protective arm about the child.

Then all of a sudden Laurel, pointing toward a small child across the park leaped down off the bench, and called happily. "There's Toddy! Oh, can we ask her to have lunch with us? Toddy! Toddy, over here!" she shouted, waving her arms.

The two girls were so happy to see each other, they flung their arms around each other and jumped up and down. Ava and Dr. Woodward smilingly watched the reunion. When they found that Toddy had been left on her own by the Hales' maid, they immediately invited her to join them.

The girls chattered excitedly, so fast that their words tumbled out, overlapping the other's. Ava watched them fondly remarking to Lee, "The dear little things. How much they must have to talk about. Laurel says nothing about her life before the Orphan Train, but I'm sure there are sad memories for all the children."

"Well, they look happy enough now," Dr. Woodward commented.

"Yes, I know, but —"

Leland took Ava's hand, raised it to his lips, and kissed it. "Better not to dwell on the sad part, my dear. Laurel has a brand new life with us now. Children soon forget the past."

"I suppose you're right," Ava said, but her eyes lingered on the two little girls, their heads close together.

A few minutes later they were diverted by the arrival of the Hansen family. This would not ordinarily have attracted the Woodwards' attention except for the fact that both Toddy and Laurel scrambled to their feet and hand in hand ran toward another little girl who had come with the Hansens. Ava saw that she was taller than the other two, with smooth brown braids. To Ava's shocked surprise, however, she was still wearing the drab dress and pinafore assigned by the orphanage!

Soon, Laurel came running over to ask if Kit could eat lunch with them, too.

"Of course," Ava smiled. A minute later Laurel returned with a disappointed face, saying Mrs. Hansen needed Kit to help serve their lunch.

"Well, perhaps she can come over later for lemonade and cake," suggested Ava, wondering why the Hansen woman couldn't see that the three little orphans needed this time to be together. Mrs. Hale had already rendered an invitation through Toddy for Laurel to come watch the fireworks display from their upstairs balcony. *She* certainly understood.

Kit, a sweet, shy child did come over later, and seeing the trio so happy together encouraged Ava to do something. She decided she would speak to Mrs. Hansen herself about allowing Kit to come, offering to drive Kit home to their farm afterward.

So, when one of the Hansens' boys came over to get Kit after she had only been with the other two a half hour, Ava walked over to where the Hansens were picnicking, and introducing herself, made her plea.

But Ava's persuasion failed to work on Mrs. Hansen who shook her head.

"No, Kit has to come with the rest of us," she said firmly.

"But the children are so looking forward to it. Surely you wouldn't want to deprive Kit of a chance to be with her friends after such a long separation —" Ava protested.

But Mrs. Hansen raised her chin defensively and her mouth was set in a stubborn line. "Kit has chores to do before it gets dark, Miz Woodward. We're gettin' set to leave now" was her reply.

Ava saw that no extension of her considerable charm would work on the woman, so she sighed and turned to leave. Seeing Kit's expression, she impulsively took the child's face in both hands. Leaning down, she kissed her cheek. "There'll be another time, Kit, I promise. We'll plan to have you come visit Laurel very soon."

Later she fumed to Lee. "What a shame, disappointing Kit like that. How can people be so insensitive?"

"She's a different kind of person from you, Ava, doesn't see things the same way."

"But to treat a child like that —"

"None of the Hansen children seem abused to me, my dear, and Kit looked fine," Leland said in an attempt to placate his wife. But he kept to himself his own concern that had sprung up the day he saw that Jess Hansen was taking Kit home with him. The child looked too delicate for heavy farm chores . . . but then, what could they do about it?

Ava bit her lower lip in frustration. She had seen something in Kit's eyes that haunted her. No matter what, she was going to do something to help the child.

8

One afternoon in early September, Leland looked in the door of Ava's sitting room. Every surface and space was covered with all sorts of fabric in a melee of color and pattern.

Glancing up, Ava saw him and motioned him into the room.

"What's all this? A circus?" he asked in amazement.

Laurel, who was sitting in a pile of jumbled cloth, giggled as she always did at Dr. Woodward's jokes.

Ava gave him a distracted glance and held up a length of material she was examining. "No, silly, we're choosing material for Laurel's school clothes. Mrs. Danby is coming tomorrow and it's going to be a week of selecting patterns, cutting and fitting and pinning. You are going to be completely surrounded by sewing women!"

"A circus! I was right." Dr. Woodward struck his head in mock horror. "Maybe I'd better take the week off and go fishing."

"Nothing of the kind, Lee. We need your opinion on some of these outfits," Ava said, pretending to be stern. "You have excellent taste."

"Mrs. Danby doesn't think so!" he declared. "The last time she was here for a week of sewing, she glared at me every time I ventured near. I think she thought I was going to perform surgery on her precious sewing machine."

At this, Laurel rolled over in a fit of giggles.

Dr. Woodward raised his eyebrows. "At least, someone appreciates me."

"I appreciate you, too, Lee. Didn't I just say as much?" Ava said. Then holding up a colorful swatch, she asked, "What do you think of this?"

He came over and took the piece and draped it about Ava's head and shoulders, then stepped back to admire her.

"Lovely! Pink is *your* color. I've always loved you in it," he said. "The first time I ever saw you you were wearing pink."

Ava smiled at him indulgently. "Actually, it was a dusty rose dress I was wearing — and *this* is coral."

"Whatever it was, you were ravishing in it," he said in a gentle, teasing voice, and leaned over to kiss her uplifted face.

For a moment they looked at each other, then at Laurel and both of them smiled, holding out their arms to her. She scrambled over the mountain of material and was drawn into the circle of their embrace.

"I'd better get out of here and let you ladies get on with whatever it is you're doing," Dr. Woodward said and started toward the door.

Ava, preoccupied with her choices once more, was holding up the rosy material to Laurel. "This will be such a becoming color for you. We'll have Mrs. Danby make it up into a little suit with a short jacket and lace collar. Oh, it will be perfect! And you will be the prettiest little girl in the whole school!"

Hearing Ava's happy chatter, Leland paused at the doorway, turning to see his wife give Laurel an impulsive hug. It gladdened his heart to see her so happy. She was completely absorbed in readying the child's wardrobe for school. It was her nature, he knew, to throw herself into a project. Yes, whatever it was — joy or grief — Ava was apt to plunge right into it!

As he made his way slowly down the stairs, he felt the vague stirring of uneasiness. As a doctor, Leland knew the danger of that kind of intensity, the extremes of emotional highs and lows to which his wife was prone. Now Laurel had become the focus of Ava's concentrated time, attention, devotion.

But wasn't this new interest in life, this enthusiastic acceptance of Laurel exactly what he had hoped would happen? Why, then had a tiny seed of fear planted itself within him and taken uneasy root there?

Mrs. Danby, the town's best seamstress, arrived on the dot of eight o'clock the next morning and took possession of the upstairs spare room. There she and Ava made the final decisions about patterns, materials and trimmings. Soon her big sewing scissors were slashed authoritatively into the cloth with a sureness that would have unnerved anyone lacking her expertise.

Laurel stood patiently while Mrs. Danby, a tape measure around her neck and her mouth full of straight pins, knelt on the floor draping, tucking, hemming, all the while with tight-lipped murmurs and grunts and little pushes, indicating which way she wanted Laurel to turn.

The result of all this week-long activity was a complete new wardrobe for Laurel.

Besides four new school dresses, there was a Sunday-best outfit and blouses, jumpers, skirts, and jackets, as well as new camisoles, petticoats, and bloomers.

On the first morning of school, Laurel was late coming down to breakfast and Dr. Woodward sent Jenny upstairs to see what was delaying her.

When Jenny walked into her room, Laurel was still in her petticoat, staring into the open armoire filled with her new clothes.

"My land, Laurel, you'll have all the other girls green with envy!" remarked Jenny in awe, thinking her own little sisters and brothers were lucky to have a couple of hand-me-downs and a new pair of sturdy boots to start school. "So what are you planning to wear?"

Laurel turned a stricken face to Jenny. "I don't *know* —"

There had never been any choice at Greystone and before that, Mama had always laid out her clothes for her to put on in the morning.

"Didn't Mrs. Woodward say what you were to wear?" Jenny asked.

Laurel shook her head.

"Well, come on then, I'll help you. You mustn't be late the first day of school now. What would your teacher say if you come in like the ten o'clock scholar in the nursery rhyme?" Jenny bustled over to the armoire, studied its contents with a slight shake of her head, then pulled out a bright blue dress trimmed with darker blue braid. She held it up for Laurel's approval. "How about this? Here, then, let me help you."

Jenny slipped it over Laurel's head, guided her arms into the sleeves, and proceeded to button the dozen small buttons in the back. When she got to the top, Laurel's chain caught and Jenny fumbled to untangle it. As she struggled unsuccessfully to free the chain or to get the button into the opening, she said, "I'd better unfasten this clasp, Laurel."

"No!" exclaimed Laurel sharply, jerking away from Jenny both hands on her neck, holding the chain.

Startled, Jenny stared at her. "Whatever is the matter? I was just —"

"I can't ever take this chain off! Not ever!" Laurel shook her head vehemently.

"I meant just until I got the top button done." Jenny explained, puzzled by Laurel's reaction. When she saw the child's eyes fill with tears, she thought, *Why she's afraid! Probably about going to school the first day.* But Laurel's next words surprised her.

"I can't take this off, Jenny, because Mama told me not to."

"But Mrs. Woodward would understand that we —"

"I don't mean *her! She's* not my *mama*," Laurel said in a low voice. With that, she took a step closer to Jenny, pulled the chain out and held up the small, heart-shaped locket. Opening it, she held it up for Jenny to see the pictures inside. "*This* is my *real* mama, and this is my *real* father."

Jenny studied the faces of the lovely, dark-eyed young woman, the handsome, serious young man, then Laurel's small, anxious one. Her thoughts were mixed. She thought of her mistress whose whole life had changed since the coming of this little girl, and of Dr. Woodward who already adored her. What would they think if they had seen the quick, possessive way Laurel had challenged the idea that either of them were her *real* mother or father?

"I'm sorry, Jenny," Laurel said quietly. "I didn't mean to yell at you."

"All right, dearie, never mind. Turn around now, and I'll do the buttons carefully so as not to catch the chain again. We'll have to hurry now. Dr. Lee is waitin' to drive you over to school."

Jenny was in the kitchen with Ella when the doctor drove off with Laurel sitting beside him in the buggy, both of them waving to Ava who stood on the porch waving her handkerchief as they left.

Unconsciously Jenny shook her head. People were already saying the Woodwards were spoiling their "little orphan." Not that Jenny agreed. She had never seen a child spoiled by too much love or caring. What bothered her now was whether Laurel would ever be able to love them back enough.

It was a strange situation, Jenny thought to herself as she began her dusting. There was still that closed door upstairs that had belonged to the Woodwards' *real* daughter, Dorie. Just as there was that locket where Laurel kept her *real* parents.

Laurel's heart was hammering as she entered Meadowridge Grammar School's fenced schoolyard, filled with boisterous children. Her hand tightened on the handle of her lunch pail, and she felt her mouth go dry when she tried to swallow. The distance from the gate over to the school building looked so far, and if she made it over there, how would she ever find the right classroom?

At the moment she was about to panic, Laurel heard someone calling her name. Turning, she was grateful to see Toddy, red-gold curls flying, running toward her across the crowded playground.

"Laurel!" Toddy came up to her smiling and breathless, holding out her hand to clasp Laurel's. "I'm so glad to see you! Let's wait here and see if Kit comes," she suggested.

At once Laurel sighed with relief. When Kit came, everything really would be all right. The three of them would be together again.

9

Christmas 1894

The Christmas program put on by the school-children in the church social hall was a great success. Everyone said so, parents congratulating Miss Cady and complimenting each other on performances of their offspring. Ava, basking in the many comments on Laurel's solo of "O Holy Night," clutched Leland's arm excitedly and whispered, "Lee, we must see that Laurel has singing lessons! Her voice is surely a God-given gift."

Unaware of the plans for her future already spinning forward in Ava's mind, Laurel found Kit and Toddy and the three of them settled together in one corner to enjoy the refreshments and compare notes about the coming holiday week.

"I'm so thankful I didn't miss a line of your poem, Kit!" Toddy gave an exaggerated sigh of relief as she forked up a large bite of applesauce cake.

"You read it so well, Toddy. You made it sound much better than I thought it was when I wrote it," Kit told her. "And Laurel, you didn't seem a bit nervous doing your song."

"I *was*, though. I thought my voice sounded shaky on the first few notes," confessed Laurel, glad that it was over.

"No school for ten whole days! And if it keeps on snowing, we can go sledding!" Toddy said with a little bounce.

"I don't have a sled," Laurel said.

"Well, you'll probably get one for Christmas." Toddy nodded her head confidently. "Bob Pennifold's father . . . you know, he runs Pennifold's Hardware Store . . . and he said a lot of folks have put in orders for sleds to give their children for presents."

"Oh, well, maybe," agreed Laurel, brightening.

Kit did not say anything. She knew there would be no such things as sleds for Christmas at the Hansens' farm.

Soon people began searching for their wraps and boots as they prepared to leave. Ava called Laurel over, handed her the new white sheared rabbit fur tam and muff. The set was "an early Christmas present," Ava had told her when she had given it to her that evening.

Toddy made both girls promise they would come over the first day after Christmas to see the Hales' tree. Its tip touched the ceiling of the parlor, she told them, and was decorated with ornaments Mrs. Hale had ordered from a store in San Francisco. Just then, Helene and Mrs. Hale called to her and Toddy went off to join them. Kit left to say goodnight to Miss Cady and Laurel, tucking her hands into her muff, walked out with the Woodwards.

Coming out into the cold, starry night from the warmth of the church social hall, the air rang with cheerful voices calling out "Merry Christmas!" as people found their buggies and wagons, and gathered their children for the ride home.

Dr. Woodward helped Ava and Laurel into theirs and tucked a warm rug over their knees. Snow was still falling gently, slowly covering the rooftops of houses and lawns along the way home, muting the sound of the horse's hoofs and buggy wheels on the snow-softened road.

"Tired, darling?" Ava asked, putting her arm around Laurel's shoulder and drawing her close.

Laurel nodded, but she really wasn't as

tired as she was preoccupied with her own thoughts. The Woodwards had set up their tree in the parlor on Sunday when Dr. Woodward was home and could help. He mostly supervised Laurel's and Ava's hanging of the ornaments and then finally climbed up the ladder to place the glittery star at the top.

Before they left for the Christmas program that evening Laurel noticed some brightly wrapped packages had already been placed underneath the tree. Laurel had been busy for weeks making her presents — an embroidered glove case for Ava and four finely hemmed linen handkerchiefs for Leland with his initials satin-stitched in the corner. They lay, prettily wrapped and hidden in her bottom drawer. She had been wondering how to get them under the tree without anyone seeing her. As soon as they got home the opportunity presented itself.

"Would you like a cup of cocoa, Laurel?" Ava asked her as they came into the house. "I'm going to make some. I got quite chilled on the drive home."

"No, thank you. I had the hot spiced cider after the program. I think I'll go get ready for bed," Laurel replied and she kissed Ava good night and went upstairs.

What luck! she thought. She would wait

until they were both safely in the kitchen having cocoa, then she would slip downstairs and put her gifts under the tree.

Ava was still standing at the bottom of the stairs, lost in thought, when Leland came in the door after taking care of his horse. He came up behind her and put his arms around her waist, leaning his cold cheek against hers for a minute.

"Oh, Leland! Laurel is such a treasure. We are so blessed." Ava sighed happily.

"I couldn't agree more, my dear."

"And with the voice of an angel."

"She sang very nicely indeed."

"Nicely? Is that all you have to say about it?"

"Well, I'm no music critic."

"You don't have to be to recognize talent like that."

"Didn't I hear you say something about making some hot cocoa?" Leland asked mildly.

"Yes, but don't change the subject." Ava removed her hat and veil, placed them on the hall table while Leland helped her off with her fur-collared cape. "We must see that Laurel's voice is properly trained." Eyeing her reflection in the hall mirror, she patted her hair absentmindedly then turned around with a small frown. "Whom should I ask about a voice teacher for her, do you suppose? Mr. Fordyce, the music teacher at the high school?"

"I'm sure I have no idea." Leland shook his head. "There's plenty of time for that."

"No, not really, Lee. It is important to start early, I've read. See that she doesn't acquire any bad habits, doesn't strain her vocal cords, learns to breathe correctly, that sort of thing."

"Laurel's only twelve, darling," Lee protested gently.

"It's soon enough. It may even be a little late!"

"Well, that may be so, my dear."

"I'm sure I'm right about the necessity of nurturing a natural gift like hers."

"Well, nothing has to be decided tonight," Leland murmured.

"You think I'm being silly, don't you?" Ava accused.

"No, not silly, my dear. Maybe just overestimating Laurel's talent *and* her desire. Maybe Laurel won't even be interested in developing her voice. Maybe, she'd rather do something else entirely."

"But it's up to us as *parents* to guide her in what's best for her. We have a responsibility to see that Laurel appreciates her gift and does whatever is necessary to cultivate it."

Ava's tone became higher, more intense. "You must not have heard all the comments I heard tonight about Laurel's singing. Everyone was so complimentary, marveling at the quality of her voice." She faced him, eyes flashing. "She *has* a gift, Leland, and I intend to see that she doesn't waste it!"

"Fine, my dear," Leland said soothingly, seeing how excited his wife was becoming. "Come along, how about the cocoa you promised?" and Leland took her hand, leading her toward the kitchen at the back of the house.

Unknown to either of them, Laurel, standing at the top of the staircase, her packages in her arms, had heard their conversation.

As their voices faded away, her hand went unconsciously to the delicate chain she always wore and she fingered the heart-shaped locket. The familiar sadness swept over her. Mama had seemed very close to her tonight, especially when she was singing.

Ever since she was a very little girl, Laurel had known all the Christmas carols. She could recall clearly sitting beside Mama at the piano while she played and sang all the lovely old songs, and Laurel had sung along with her.

Christmas was always a special time in that small apartment at the top of Mrs. Campbell's house, even though they had only a tiny tree set on the table and a few little gifts. It was special because Mama made it so. Laurel closed her eyes and she could almost see it all again — the candles' glow, the sound of the piano, Mama's beautiful smile, her graceful hands moving over the keys —

Laurel loved to sing, knew that when she sang she felt a soaring sensation, as if a part of herself left and became one with the song, with the music. She remembered Mama saying, "Why Laurel, you sound just like a little lark!"

When she sang it was always for her — for Mama.

10

The Class of 1900

Laurel stood at the hall mirror retying the bow at the collar of her pink shirtwaist when Dr. Woodward came downstairs and stopped behind her.

"Good morning, my dear, you look as fresh as a daisy," he complimented her. "All ready for the Senior Picnic, are you?"

"Yes, Papa Lee." Laurel whirled around to greet him. "I'm waiting for Dan. He'll be here in a few minutes. We'll walk over to school and meet the rest of the class. There will be hay wagons to take us out to Riverview Park for the picnic."

"That sounds like fun." Dr. Woodward smiled. "Well, I have office hours this morning, so I'd better get out there. Have a good time."

"We will, Papa, thanks," Laurel assured him, offering her soft cheek for his kiss.

Leland went out the side door, stopped in the garden to pick a rosebud from one of his wife's prized bushes to put in the lapel of his tan linen jacket, then proceeded to his small office at the back of the house.

At three months past fifty, Leland was still handsome, with well-defined features and a pleasant smile. There was more silver in his thick wavy hair now, but with his erect, lean build, he had the appearance of a much younger man.

A few minutes later, standing at his office window, he watched Laurel and Dan Brooks go out the front gate together. Fondly, his eyes followed Laurel's graceful figure and the lanky one of the tall boy at her side as they turned in the direction of Meadowridge High School.

He was pleased that Laurel was going to their class picnic with Dan. He liked the young fellow. Of all the boys whose bicycles had cluttered up the front walk since Laurel was about fifteen, or who had parked themselves on the front porch, bringing valentines or flowers, boxes of candy and Christmas gifts, Dan was Leland's favorite.

If he had had a son of his own, Leland would have wanted one like Dan. The boy was courteous, intelligent, dependable. He could carry on a decent conversation with an adult, which was more than Leland could say for half of those who had stood tongue-tied and awkwardly ill at ease in the Woodwards' hallway, waiting for Laurel to come down and rescue them.

Leland only hoped Laurel had the good sense to recognize Dan's good qualities and appreciate them. Maybe in a few years things would develop between them and become more than a friendship. Of course, they were still very young, plenty of time to think of the future.

Just then looking up at Dan, Laurel's head tilted sideways, and Leland could see her enchanting profile — the small sweet nose, the slender neck above the ruffled edge of her high-necked blouse. Just this week, in anticipation of her official entry into young womanhood via graduation, Laurel had begun pinning up her dark, wavy hair. It made her look very grown up.

Unconsciously, Leland sighed. Was it possible it had been ten years since as a seven-year-old child, Laurel had come into their home?

"Lee, still alone? No patients yet?"

Ava's voice interrupted his thoughts and Leland turned to see her face peering around the office door.

"Yes, I mean, no — I'm alone, no patients.

Come in, darling," Leland invited.

Ava slipped in, closing the door quietly behind her.

Looking at her, Leland was struck, as he always was, that she seemed to grow lovelier with each passing year. Her figure was still girlishly slim, the dark hair still untouched by a single strand of gray, her skin pale and smooth, translucent as fine porcelain. Of course, since Laurel had come into their lives, they both seemed rejuvenated.

At the moment, however, a small anxious frown cast two vertical lines between Ava's dark, winged brows. Her expression alerted him that something was troubling her. A tiny twinge of concern stirred, tightening his chest. Ava tended to get upset about small, unimportant things. What was it now?

Leland went over to her, took both her hands in his, and was startled to feel they were icy.

"What is it, Ava, what's wrong?"

"Did you see Laurel?" she asked.

"Yes, right before she left. She looked charming, as usual."

"Yes, that pale pink blouse is so becoming —" Ava said with a distracted air, then rushed on. "Did you see her leave with *that* boy?"

"With Dan? Yes, of course, why?"

"*Why?* That's why I'm so upset. He's taken her to every single graduation event. *That's* what upsets me. He's totally unsuitable."

"Unsuitable?" Leland repeated in surprise. "How do you mean *unsuitable?* I think he's a capital young chap. What do you mean?"

"His *family,* Leland, *that's* what I mean."

"There's nothing wrong with the family, as far as I know. His grandmother and aunts are patients of mine. They're members of the church. They're fine ladies. I don't know what you're talking about."

"I *know* he lives with *them,* Leland, and everything looks very respectable, but —" Ava lowered her voice. "His mother lives in Chicago and his father, well, no one seems to know much about him. But the *brother,* Dan's *uncle, is Ned Morris* —" Ava broke off in dismay. "Surely, you know he runs a pool hall on the other side of town."

Leland started to laugh. Shaking his head he protested, "But, darling, what's that got to do with Dan? He lives with Mrs. Morris over on Elm Street —"

"Leland, you're purposely trying not to understand." Ava sounded exasperated. "I just don't want Laurel associating with that sort of person."

It was Leland's turn to be irritated.

"Laurel isn't associating with Dan's uncle, my dear, so I don't see the problem."

Ava hesitated a moment before answering.

"The boy is obviously in love with Laurel. Doesn't *that* disturb you?"

"In love? At *their* age?" Leland scoffed. "They aren't even out of high school yet."

"They will be in a week, must I remind you, and then —"

"Ava, my dear, you're borrowing trouble. Besides, Dan told me he has applied to medical school. He's got long years of study ahead. He hasn't time to be serious about anything but getting his education. I *know* what that's like. It will be a long time before he can think about anything else."

Ava seemed somewhat appeased. "I just don't want him getting any ideas about Laurel," she went on. "You know how she is. I'm afraid he might convince her to make some kind of promise about the future —"

"Be sensible, Ava. You must be imagining things. I haven't noticed Laurel treating Dan in any special way. No more than any of the other young men who've come calling. Laurel doesn't even see as much of him as she does her girl friends, Toddy and Kit. I believe you're worrying unnecessarily. Besides, I don't think Laurel would keep anything as important as being in love from *us.*"

"I suppose you're right, Leland," Ava sighed. "You usually are!"

Leland put his arms around her, held her. "Sweetheart, you must not fret about things that may never be! Remember the Scripture, "Sufficient unto the day," he said soothingly. "Now, why don't you find something better to do than worry about two youngsters who have nothing on their minds but having a wonderful day at a picnic?"

"Laurel, I love you," Dan whispered.

"Oh, Dan, I wish you wouldn't say that," Laurel protested softly.

"But, it's true. You must know it, Laurel. Why can't I say it?"

After the delicious picnic prepared by the mothers of the Junior Class and served by rising Meadowridge Seniors, most of the "honorees" had paired off and left the picnic area, to roam along the wooded paths through the park or to follow the trail down to the river.

Dan and Laurel had climbed up the hillside to the meadow overlooking the river and had settled under the shade of a gnarled, ancient oak. The afternoon seemed to stretch endlessly under a lapis lazuli sky. The hum of insects among the wildflowers in the tall grass floated on sweet-scented summer air. The sun was a drowsy warmth. For a while Dan lay on his stomach, gazing at Laurel, wondering if she had any idea what a picture she made. What was she thinking about?

Laurel leaned her head back against the tree, feeling the roughness of its bark through the thin material of her blouse and camisole.

With eyes half-closed, Laurel could see Dan, his head turned so that his clear-cut profile was outlined against the cloudless blue background of the sky. Her mind drifted aimlessly and she began to mentally rehearse the lyrics of the song she was to sing at the Honors Banquet.

It was then that Dan had raised himself to a sitting position, reached for her hand, brought it to his lips and kissed the tips of her fingers.

When he declared, "I love you, Laurel," she tried to pull her hand away, but Dan held it fast.

"Why is it wrong for me to say what I've felt all these months . . . for years actually. I guess it's just *this* year I realized what it's going to be like when I go away to medical school next fall and won't be able to see you every day."

Laurel met his earnest, brown eyes and felt her own heart respond to what he was saying, but at the same time she was afraid. She knew "Mother" did not like Dan and she felt torn between her two loyalties, not knowing how to explain one to the other without betraying either of them.

"What I want to know, Laurel, is do you care for me?" Dan's voice was intense, pleading. "I mean *really* care, more than just a friend, more than anyone else . . . enough to wait . . . until I finish my training, become a doctor? I know that's a long time, an awful lot to ask. But, Laurel, I don't know how I can go off next fall, leave Meadowridge and not know that you — that you —"

"Oh, Dan, I *do* care, but I don't think you should talk like this. We're both . . . well, we're just getting out of high school. We have our whole lives ahead of us. Don't you think it's too early for us to make plans, or promises?"

"Don't you ever daydream about the future, Laurel? Wonder what it will be like to make our own decisions, our own choices?"

"Of course, I do —" began Laurel, then stopped short. Of course, she daydreamed but she had never shared those daydreams with anyone. Laurel had always had a "secret life" filled with dreams and plans about the future. But, mostly, she lived in the present, drifting from day to day, trying to please everyone, trying to make "Mother" and Papa Lee happy, proud of her.

Like with her music. "Mother" was always so interested in the new songs Mr. Fordyce gave her to learn, so thrilled every time Laurel was asked to perform. Ava always had Laurel sing for her Sewing Circle when it met at the Woodwards' but "Mother" never guessed how nervous it made Laurel to sing for an audience, how much it cost her to meet those expectations.

And now Dan was pressuring her, wanting her to make a commitment to him. Gently, Laurel withdrew her hand.

"Dan, it's too soon for us to make any promises. Can't you be satisfied to know I *do* care very much about you? Isn't that enough for now?"

Dan sighed heavily. "I guess it will *have* to be."

He got to his feet, walked over to the cliff, bent down and picked up some small stones and stood tossing them down into the river below. Laurel looked over at his tall figure, the shoulders drooping slightly with disappointment. Then she leaned back against the tree again and closed her eyes.

Sometimes she wished she could go away

somewhere where no one expected anything of her at all. She let her mind wander back to that old fantasy, the one kept locked in her heart all these years, the story she used to tell herself at night when she was lying in bed not quite ready to go to sleep.

It was then she planned how, when she grew up and finished school, she would go back to Boston and find Mrs. Campbell's old house. She would ring the doorbell and Mrs. Campbell would come to the door. Seeing her, her old landlady would throw up her hands and say, "Why, land's sake, if it isn't Laurel Vestal, all grown up!" Then she would take Laurel upstairs to their old apartment, unlock the door, and Laurel would walk inside and everything would be just the same as the last time she had seen it.

Laurel would go through it, room by room, remembering — the upright piano with the candleholders on either side of the music rack with her father's painting of the lighthouse hanging over it, her mother's rocker over by the window with the little footstool where Laurel used to sit. In the bedroom, Laurel would picture the trundle bed they pulled out from under her Mama's high poster, and in the corner the table with the lamp and the books —

Sometimes, at this point, Laurel would fall asleep. But the next night and the night after that, she would begin her journey again. The longer she was with the Woodwards, the less she had done that. But today it all came back to her as clearly and vividly as ever.

It was not that Laurel was unhappy. Her life at the Woodwards could not have been happier or more pleasant. It would have been hard to find a more loving, caring atmosphere for a child to grow up in.

But all through the years, Laurel had clung to her memories like a drowning person clutching at a straw, as if by letting go, she would drift down the stream, be swept into the rushing current, and lose something vital. Lose her other life, that life with Mama that filled her with such sweet longing and sadness.

Why could she not let it go? Was it because it had taken her so long to accept that her mama had really died? For weeks she had refused to believe it. Mama had promised she would come back —

Of course, eventually, the reality had penetrated. Still, buried deep in her child's heart was the determination that one day she would go back and find that lost part of herself.

"Come on, Laurel. Everyone's starting

back. They're loading up the wagons to go back into town!"

"Wake up, Laurel!"

Toddy's voice broke into Laurel's thoughts, and she opened her eyes, blinking into the sunshine. Toddy and Chris Blanchard were standing over her.

"We just came up from the river," Toddy said, holding up her white cotton stockings and shoes. "We went wading!" Then, pointing to the hem of her bedraggled skirt, she made a face. "Miss Klitgard will look daggers at me! So very *unladylike*, Miss Hale!" she declared, mimicking one of their teacher-chaperones for the picnic.

It was such an exact imitation they all laughed.

Joining in, Dan held out his hands to Laurel and pulled her to her feet. "Time to go!" Then, hand in hand, they walked back down the hill to the picnic area where the wagons for the ride back to town were loading.

As the three wagons, drawn by plodding farm horses and filled with young people singing at the top of their voices, lumbered into the school yard, passers-by on Elm Street smiled nostalgically, recalling their own bygone youth.

In one last exuberant burst of song, the strains of the school song echoed through

115

the early evening air: "Forever we'll remember thee, Meadowridge High, we'll
faithful be!" and ended with riotous
laughter and clapping hands.

Dan jumped down from the end of the
wagon and held up his arms to Laurel, who
placed her hands on his shoulders. Lifting
her down, he held her a moment longer than
necessary. "I'll walk you home," he whispered.

"Oh, you don't need to, Dan. It's still
light. Besides, don't you have to get to
work?" Laurel asked, knowing Dan had a
job at the pharmacy three nights a week.

"I have time," he assured her, planning to
skip supper in order to make it to his job by
six.

"You're sure?" Laurel sounded doubtful.

"Yes," Dan told her, drawing her hand
through his arm as they started out of the
school yard.

Toddy and Chris, heading toward the
Hale house, called and waved as they went
in the other direction.

"I *can* take you to the Honors Banquet tomorrow night, can't I, Laurel?" Dan asked
on the way home.

Laurel hesitated. "I don't know, Dan.
Papa Lee and Mother plan to attend and I
think they expect me to go with them."

He frowned. "Well, I realize parents will be there, Laurel, but our whole class will have its own table and —"

"Maybe I'd just better wait and see —" Her voice trailed off uncertainly.

Dan knew better than to persist, but his jaw tightened.

They said nothing more until they reached the Woodwards' white picket fence. Dan opened the gate for her and they went through into the back garden, fragrant now with June roses.

"About the Banquet, Laurel —" he began.

"I told you I'd have to see, Dan," Laurel reminded him gently.

Dan did not want to argue about it. Anything to do with Laurel's parents' wishes always presented a problem. He'd run into that barrier often enough before.

"I know, but I'd just like to know —"

"I understand. But if Mother and Papa Lee want me —" Laurel sighed softly. It was so hard to explain to anyone, even Dan, how easily Mother's feelings were hurt.

Just then they heard the squeak of the screen door opening and Mrs. Woodward came out onto the back porch, a slim figure in a filmy white dress. She walked to the edge of the steps, peering into the gathering lavender dusk.

"Oh, there you are, Laurel darling!" she called. "I was getting worried. It's nearly five-thirty. I thought you'd be home way before now. I was afraid there might have been an accident . . . those narrow country roads and those top-heavy wagons —"

Laurel moved quickly away from Dan and took a few steps forward so Ava could see her.

"No, Mother, everything's fine! Nothing happened! I'm sorry you were worried."

"Oh, well, as long as you're home safe!" Mrs. Woodward sounded relieved. "Come along, I'll run a nice tub for you. You must be tired after such a long day."

"I'll be there in just a minute. Dan's here. He walked me home."

"Hello, Mrs. Woodward." Dan stepped into Mrs. Woodward's line of vision.

"Oh, hello, Dan." There was a definite coolness in Ava's voice.

Laurel winced inwardly. Why did Mother always ignore Dan unless he made it a point to force her to see him, speak to him? He had never mentioned this to her, but it was so obvious, it hurt Laurel for him.

"Well, come along, Laurel, or your bath water will get cold." Mrs. Woodward disappeared into the house.

"I'll have to go in." Laurel turned to Dan.

"It was such a nice day. Thanks for seeing me home." As she put her foot on the first step of the porch, Dan caught her hand and held it.

They stood for a long minute in the soft twilight, looking at each other. Laurel drew in her breath. She saw something in Dan's eyes that both stirred and frightened her.

Withdrawing her hand, she said breathlessly, "Good night, Dan," and ran lightly up the steps and into the house.

11

On the afternoon of the Honors Banquet, Laurel walked over to the high school for her final rehearsal of the songs she was to sing that night and at the graduation ceremony.

This last week of the school year, the building was nearly empty. A few students were sitting in the sunshine looking at the yearbook when Laurel went up the steps and inside. As she walked down the deserted corridor, she heard the sound of a trumpet solo being played haltingly. She opened the door to the Music Room and quietly took a seat at the back. The boy with the trumpet struggled on valiantly until Mr. Fordyce spoke to him.

"That's enough for today, Billy. You need some practice, young fellow. Guess we've had too much baseball weather lately, eh?" He tousled the youngster's hair affectionately. "But I expect you to know that piece by heart next week."

"Yes, sir," the boy mumbled getting to his feet. There was much scuffling and clatter as he packed his instrument in its carrying case and hurried out into what was left of the beautiful afternoon.

Then Mr. Fordyce looked over, acknowledged Laurel's presence, and beckoned her forward while he took his place at the piano. Mr. Fordyce had given Laurel private lessons for years, and she considered him a friend.

"All right now, Laurel, let's begin with scales before we go into your numbers."

Laurel adjusted the music stand, placed her music sheets on it and, when Mr. Fordyce struck the first note, she took a deep breath and began.

Less than an hour later, Mr. Fordyce stopped playing and announced, "There, that's it. I think we're through for today. You can over-rehearse, you know."

Laurel was surprised. Usually Mr. Fordyce made many corrective comments, made her go over and over her pieces. Now he stood up, gathered his music, shut the lid over the keyboard.

"Then, it sounded all right?" she asked doubtfully.

"It was fine, Laurel. You'll do splendidly, I'm sure."

Laurel hesitated, there was something in the way he spoke that vaguely troubled her. She stood by the piano uncertainly. She felt there was something he was *not* saying that was more important than what he had said.

"Mr. Fordyce?"

"Yes, Laurel."

"Did I do something wrong?"

"No, not at all, Laurel. Everything was fine, on pitch, on key. Be sure and rest your voice for the next few hours. Drink some hot lemonade before the performance."

"There's nothing else you wanted to say to me?" she persisted.

Mr. Fordyce continued busily stacking music sheets, then he turned toward her, his face thoughtful. "I guess, I was just wondering what your plans are for after graduation."

"I'm not sure —" she said.

Mr. Fordyce opened his briefcase and began stuffing the music sheets inside. When he looked up again, his face was serious, his eyes grave as he regarded her.

"No plans, eh? What about your voice?"

"I do want to continue my lessons through the summer —" she told him, smiling tentatively. "That is, if you —"

"Laurel! I didn't mean just this summer!" He sounded irritated. "You *have* a voice, you know. Don't you care about it? I know dozens of others who would die for what you have." He sighed heavily. "Laurel, I've taught you all I can. I can't do any more to help you develop your voice. There's so much you still need to know, to learn. But you can't do it here in Meadowridge. There's no one here who has what you need."

Laurel stared at him.

Again Mr. Fordyce sounded annoyed.

"But you have to *know* that, not have me *tell* you. You have to *want* it for yourself. Some things cannot be taught. For a singer there has to be something inside that tells her she has to go on, that she will *die* if she cannot learn everything there is to learn, to seek to be the best she can be with the talent she's been given." He stopped, shook his head. "If you don't have that desire, Laurel, well, what more can I say?"

"But where could I go? Who could I find to teach me?"

"You'd have to go somewhere like Chicago or Boston where there is a music conservatory, where there are teachers who can give you what you need —" He paused again. "Haven't you even discussed the possibility with your parents? Surely, they could afford to send you. Your mother has always been so supportive of your singing —"

"No. I guess we just assumed I'd go on taking lessons from you, that I would sing in the choir, or for social occasions —" Her voice faltered. For some reason Laurel felt apologetic, confused, and something else she could not quite name.

"You mean singing for your friends' weddings, somebody's funeral service, for the Ladies Aid Guild meetings?" Mr. Fordyce's tone was sarcastic. He shook his head again. "Forgive me, Laurel. I've seen so much wasted talent I think I've become —" He stopped, head down, as if deep in thought. Then he raised his head and looked straight at Laurel.

"Well, Laurel, I think, after graduation, you should sit down with Dr. and Mrs. Woodward and discuss this seriously. In fact, if you like I'll come and talk to them. Suggest a school or teacher."

Laurel twisted her hands nervously. "Maybe — yes, I suppose . . . I don't really know, Mr. Fordyce. I'll have to think about it."

"Yes, I hope you will do that." Mr. Fordyce seemed weary. Then he attempted a lighter tone, "And, Laurel, don't worry about tonight. You'll do just fine. Enjoy the next few days. High school graduation is very special. There's time enough to think of the future."

"Thank you, Mr. Fordyce," Laurel murmured and, picking up her music, left.

Outside, she felt disoriented. She started walking but not in the direction of home. Instead, she turned and headed for the town park. There she found a bench near the duck pond and sat down. She realized she was trembling.

She tried to remember everything Mr. Fordyce had said, but what kept repeating itself over and over in her head were the words, "You would have to go to Chicago or *Boston* where there is a music conservatory, teachers." Was this the sign she'd been praying for? If she could go to *Boston,* then perhaps she could trace her real parents, find out about Mama's death, where she was buried, what had happened to all their things. The hope Laurel had carried for so long, hidden in her heart, burst into new life! Maybe this was the way being opened for her.

Her singing had been so much a part of her life that she had never considered it as separate from herself, as something to be developed, cared for, polished, like a rare instrument. She had sung all her life, as a little child alongside her dear mama at the piano; after coming to Meadowridge, at school and at church. Later she had sung in the choir.

It was Mother who insisted on her having lessons with Mr. Fordyce. But what Mr. Fordyce was suggesting was something different entirely. He was talking about her studying voice seriously, devoting her life to singing.

Laurel knew that something strange and wonderful happened to her when she sang. She felt a lifting, soaring sensation that carried her far beyond the room, the people, the faces of the listening audience or congregation. It was a feeling she never experienced in any other way.

Is that what Mr. Fordyce was trying to get her to express? To speak of that inner joy she felt while she was singing? Or had he meant more than that?

Yes, Laurel was sure Mr. Fordyce was looking for something else in her answer today. He was trying to see if she had that necessary desire, testing her to see if it was strong enough to make the choice of a life of total dedication.

Laurel realized that now was the time of decision. Would it be wrong to use her voice as a means to pursuing her real desire? If the Woodwards would finance her musical education in *Boston* —

Unconsciously, Laurel fingered the locket she still wore around her neck. She thought of that long-ago promise she had made to herself that, just yesterday, at the picnic, had come back to her so vividly.

Of course, Laurel knew it was foolish to suppose anything was still there. Even Mrs. Campbell might be gone. But maybe she could find out something about her father, his family, the Vestals.

Would it be deceitful to combine studying voice, which should please Mother especially, while she pursued her long-cherished dream of solving the mystery surrounding her own background?

Laurel tried imagining the discussion with Papa Lee and Mother, Mr. Fordyce had suggested. What would they say? Would they let her go?

It was too much to think about now. There was the banquet tonight, Baccalaureate service the following day, then graduation and the Graduation Dance to look forward to — Laurel rose and started walking slowly home.

She wouldn't say anything about this yet. Not tell anyone, not even Dan. There was plenty of time. The whole summer before anything would really have to be decided.

12

The evening of graduation day, Dan walked over from Elm Street to the Woodwards' house to escort Laurel to their class party. He carried with him a small corsage of sweetheart roses for her.

Before ringing the doorbell, he adjusted his tie, ran a nervous finger around the inside of the unaccustomed high, stiff shirt collar, and straightened his new navy blue jacket.

To his dismay it was Mrs. Woodward, not Laurel, who answered the door.

"Good evening, Dan," she greeted him. "How nice you look!" She smiled but there was the usual wariness in her eyes. "Do come in. You're a little early, aren't you? Laurel is not quite ready yet, which doesn't really matter, because we have to wait for Dr. Woodward. He was called out on an emergency, but he should be along soon. He wanted to see Laurel before you left for the party."

Dan tried to swallow his disappointment. All day he had been looking forward to this evening, the chance to be alone with Laurel. The early part of the day had been chaotic, with the graduation ceremony, the long program of speeches in the hot auditorium, and afterwards family and friends crowding around. The picture-taking session had dragged on endlessly. He had hardly seen Laurel.

But tonight was different. Tonight was *their* night. As graduates, they were almost adults by most standards. Tonight was their exclusive party. Even though it would be well chaperoned by teachers and some parents, Dan planned to manage having Laurel to himself for once — at least, that's what he had hoped.

"Come along, out to the side porch and have a glass of iced tea," invited Mrs. Woodward, leading the way across the parlor out through the glass doors onto the side porch.

Its white wicker furniture gleamed in the gathering twilight; the plump flowered cretonne cushions were crisp and new. On a round table in the center was a tray holding tall glasses and a crystal pitcher filled with amber liquid, aswim with lemon slices and mint leaves.

Everything at the Woodwards' was always so perfect, thought Dan, not shabby, mended and drab like his grandmother's house. All the rooms in the house on Elm Street, except for the parlor which was rarely used, needed paint, new wallpaper, new curtains, rugs or furniture. It was a very old house; it smelled old, looked old, felt old. His grandmother had been very young when her father had built it. She had been married from there, moved back into it after she was left a young widow with three little girls. Dan's mother was the only one of them who had married and left home; his two maiden aunts still lived there.

Dan was thinking about his mother when Mrs. Woodward's voice interposed, "I suppose your family is mighty proud of you, Dan. Being the class salutatorian is quite an honor."

"Yes, ma'am, it is," replied Dan, still standing awkwardly, holding Laurel's corsage, not knowing exactly where to sit.

Mrs. Woodward, occupied with pouring the tea, turned to hand him a glass when she saw his problem. "Would you like me to take the flowers up to Laurel, or would you rather just set them aside for now, and give them to her yourself?" she asked.

"Well —" he hesitated.

With a barely perceptible sigh she put the glass back on the tray and held out her hands for the corsage. "Here, we can just set them down over here. They're very pretty, Dan, but the color — I'm not sure with Laurel's dress —" her voice trailed off doubtfully. Then she added, "Well, I'm sure it won't matter, she'll appreciate them anyway." Mrs. Woodward shrugged slightly as though it were not important.

Dan felt his face grow hot. Why hadn't he thought to ask Laurel the color of her dress? All he'd thought of was how much she loved roses, and the pale yellow ones with a blush of coral seemed so right for her. But now he was unsure.

Dan tensed. Why had Mrs. Woodward had to say anything? Why did she have to spoil his pleasure? Make him feel uncertain? He felt a raw resentment rise up within him. But then, to be fair, she didn't know he had splurged his hard-earned money to buy them, or how long he'd stayed at the florist shop deciding which ones to get.

Mrs. Woodward picked up the filled glass again and, placing a small embroidered napkin under it, held it out to him.

131

Dan took it and backed up toward the chair behind him and sat down, balancing the glass carefully. He glanced cautiously in Mrs. Woodward's direction as she gracefully seated herself opposite him.

"And what are your plans now that you've graduated, Dan?" Her soft voice somehow accentuated his discomfort. He wished Laurel would come. He had never spent much time with Mrs. Woodward, and he always felt uncomfortable around the lady, even in these brief times. He cleared his throat.

"Well, I'll be working full-time for Mr. Groves at the Pharmacy for the summer, then in the fall I'll be going to college —"

"Oh, and where will that be?"

"I'll be going back to Ohio —"

"Ohio? Why is that?"

"Well, it's near my father's folks and —"

"Your father?" There was a hint of surprise in Ava's voice.

Dan's mouth felt dry. He didn't want to have to go into a long explanation about the family. It was all so complicated. All his relationships were. Even his own questions about them had never been satisfactorily answered. All he really knew was that for reasons he had never been told, his parents had lived apart since he was a little boy. His father had been in the Army and died in Cuba during the Spanish-American War. Since he was nine, Dan had lived in Meadowridge with Grandmother Morris, his aunts Sue and Vera, while his mother worked as a milliner in a big city department store.

"Yes, I'll be attending the State College and I can spend weekends with them. They have a farm, I can help out —"

Dan took a gulp of tea and felt a piece of ice lodge in the back of his throat. He worked it forward to keep from choking.

"I see," Mrs. Woodward said in a tone that implied she did not see at all.

He glanced over at her, looking cool and serene in a light flowered dress with a wide bertha collar edged in deep lace, dark hair swept back from a pale, aristocratic face.

Dan had a momentary mental picture of his mother meeting Ava Woodward. It was hard to imagine. They were so different. His mother had had a hard life, so his aunts were often fond of saying. An image of her came to Dan — the thin face, anxious eyes, her brow puckered in a perpetually worried frown. Yes, he guessed she had a lot of things to worry about, a woman struggling alone to work and support a child. And she had done that. Regularly every month a money order came to Dan's grandmother, and every fall she had sent money for his new school clothes. As Dan had "shot up like the proverbial weed," as Grandma Morris complained, the cost of his clothing went up, too. That was the reason his mother hadn't been able to afford the train fare to visit the last few years. Dan had not seen her in over a year until she had arrived for his graduation.

They had been awkward with each other after so long a time apart. They seemed to have little to say to each other. She was going to stay until the end of the week and then would be leaving again. He had felt guilty leaving her tonight. Not knowing about the long-planned graduation party, she had thought they would have a little family get-together. Even Uncle Ned was coming.

Thinking of his uncle, Dan felt self-conscious. He knew Mrs. Woodward did not approve of him, or at least of what he did. But if it weren't for Uncle Ned, many things would have been impossible for Dan. He might have even had to drop out of school at the eighth grade as so many of the fellows did to help out at home. And Uncle Ned had promised to help him with college and medical school expenses.

Just then, to Dan's immense relief, the screen door opened and Dr. Woodward came out onto the porch, saying jovially, "Well, here I am, my dear. Hello there, Dan."

Dan got to his feet as the doctor extended his hand and in doing so spilled some of his tea. Neither Dr. or Mrs. Woodward seemed to notice, and Dan quickly brushed it off his new white flannel trousers, hoping it wouldn't stain.

Desperately, he wished Laurel would hurry and come.

Upstairs, Laurel slid a filigreed silver comb, one of her graduation gifts, into her swirl of lustrous dark hair, then took a step back from the mirror to judge the effect.

"How does that look, Jenny?" she asked.

Jenny, standing alongside, waiting to help Laurel into her evening gown, nodded approvingly, "Lovely! Land sakes, Laurel, but you do look growed up, with your hair up and all."

"I'm supposed to look grown up, Jenny! I'm eighteen and finished school!" Laurel laughed, the high, sweet laugh that always reminded people of wind chimes.

"Don't seem any time since I was helping you get dressed to go to Toddy's surprise birthday party!" Jenny shook her head in disbelief.

That afternoon, as Jenny and Ella sat proudly with the Woodwards at the graduation ceremony, watching Laurel march up to receive her diploma, they had both remarked that it seemed only yesterday since Laurel was a little girl.

"Well, let's get your dress on now," Jenny suggested. "You know Dan's come, don't you?"

"Yes," Laurel said and slipped her arms into the dress Jenny was holding, then turned around so that Jenny could button the tiny satin-covered buttons down the back.

"My but this *is* a pretty dress!" Jenny nodded appreciatively as the silk voile fell in ruffled tiers over the taffeta underskirt. The delicate blue-violet material set off Laurel's coloring — her peach-bloom complexion, her dark eyes and hair. Its exquisitely embroidered bodice traced the graceful line of her shoulders, the tucked bandeau, her small waist. "You do look a picture."

Even allowing that Jenny was hopelessly prejudiced in her favor, Laurel knew the dress was flatteringly becoming. And it *was* a very grown-up dress!

"You're wearing this, aren't you?" Jenny

picked up the necklace of seed pearls and tiny amethysts from the top of the dressing table.

She saw Laurel hesitate a second. Her hand went to the chain and locket she never took off before she answered.

"I suppose Mother will wonder if I don't —" she sighed, then she tucked the locket under her dress into her chemise leaving the thin chain barely visible, and turned so that Jenny could clasp the pearl necklace around her neck.

Then Jenny handed her a small beaded purse, in which was a scented handkerchief, a small brush, some extra hairpins, a slim silver container for rice powder, a tiny vial of eau de fleur cologne, and her gloves.

"Oh, Jenny, thanks!" Laurel exclaimed. "Thanks for everything and for the lovely present, too!"

Jenny had given Laurel a scrapbook with gold printed letters on the front "Schoolday Memories."

"I thought it would be a nice thing for your keepsakes," Jenny said, pleased that Laurel seemed to like it as much as several of the expensive graduation gifts the Woodwards had given her.

"Oh, it will be just right for all my mementos . . . like this!" Laurel dangled the

137

small tassled dance card before putting it in her evening bag, too. "Thank you, Jenny. Good night!"

Laurel gave her a hug, then pirouetted across the room to the doorway, waved and went along the hall and down the stairway.

"Good night! Have a good time, Laurel!" Jenny called after her.

For some reason Jenny shivered. She didn't know why on such a balmy June evening! A strange, unwanted thought crossed Jenny's mind. What will happen to Laurel now? She did not like the cold, shuddery feeling that passed over her, and she quickly set about picking up some of Laurel's discarded clothes, hanging them up in her armoire, and then turning down her bed.

The walk from the Woodwards' to Meadowridge High had been all too short for Dan who had wanted to delay sharing Laurel as long as possible. As they strolled through the soft summer evening, he had been newly aware of everything about her — the sweet smell of her freshly washed hair, the delicate violet scent of her, the rustle of her gown. He had not wanted their time alone together to end.

But it did, just as they reached the school steps. Chris Blanchard, with Toddy coming from the other direction, greeted them. The girls immediately began to chatter, admiring each other's gowns and flowers and exchanging news about graduation gifts. Then the four of them went into the building together.

Japanese lanterns, strung from the ceiling rafters, shed mellow rosy-golden light, transforming the school auditorium. Lively music was playing and couples were already on the dance floor. Standing at the threshold the foursome was at once surrounded by their classmates, everyone in high spirits with a new sense of freedom since being graduated that afternoon.

"There's Kit!" exclaimed Toddy, waving her over to join them.

Kit, Laurel thought, had never looked so lovely. She had changed from the atrocious dress she had worn for graduation into an elegantly simple lace-trimmed blouse and slightly flared white skirt. White roses were tucked into the braided coil of her dark hair and her smooth, olive complexion was faintly flushed. Her smile was radiant and she seemed happier and more carefree than Laurel had ever seen her. And why not? She had given a superb valedictory speech and been awarded a scholarship to Merrivale Teachers College. It couldn't have happened to a nicer person, Laurel thought fondly.

Everyone clustered around Kit to congratulate her, and she laughed and accepted it all with a new sparkle.

Just then the band blared a fanfare. Mr. Dean, the athletic coach, was on the stage and held up his hand to quiet the hum of conversation to make an announcement.

"Ladies and Gentlemen . . . you noticed that *since this afternoon*, I am not addressing you as *boys and girls!*" he joked. This comment received a general laugh and a spatter of applause. He smiled and continued. "Now, you have been together as a class for four years and probably think you know each other pretty well, but, how often have you *really* talked to a member of your class who wasn't a *special* friend? Well, tonight we thought we'd give you a last chance to meet and talk to someone you might have wanted to for a long time, and were too shy, too busy or too scared to talk to before!" He held up a large box decorated in their class colors of green and gold. "In here on slips of paper are names of famous people, but separated into first name and last name. Each of you will have to find the matching part. And when you do, you and your match will have five minutes to ask questions and find out something about that person you didn't know, and vice versa!"

A buzz of comments and laughter followed this as everyone lined up to draw a slip of paper from the box.

Inwardly, Dan groaned. If this was going to be a night of party games . . . when all he wanted to do was to be with Laurel —

But when he found that the person who completed the name he had drawn — "Robin" — was Toddy, holding a slip of paper on which was written "Hood," his heart lifted in relief.

"Not fair!" she pretended to pout. "We know each other too well." She glanced around. "Shall we trade with someone else."

"Not on your life! There are lots of things I don't know about you and I mean to find out!" Dan teased. This was great! With Toddy he could relax, not have to search his mind for questions or make small talk with some girl who was practically a stranger. Dan had always been so busy with his after-school job and his studies that he had not had time to do much socializing. Actually, the only girls in his class he knew other than Laurel to speak to were Laurel's two best friends, Kit and Toddy.

"Well, then, come on," Toddy laughed, "and I'll tell you all the deep, dark secrets of my life." They found two chairs on the edge of the dance floor and sat down. "Now, I'll ask you the question everybody's been asking me most of the day. What are you going to do now that you've graduated, Dan?"

"But you know that, don't you? I'm going away to college in the fall, and then on to medical school. That is —"

"I think that is wonderful, Dan! Most of the boys don't think past college if that —" She sighed. "Take Chris —"

"*You* take him, Toddy!" Dan laughed. "It's *you* he wants."

"That's just it. Just what I'm talking about, Dan. We should all have plans, ambitions and dreams beyond Meadowridge."

"Doesn't Chris?"

"He's going to the same college his father did, then he'll come home and go into the family business."

"Are you sure? You may be selling Chris short, Toddy."

"Maybe. Maybe college will change him."

"It's bound to. College changes everyone."

Toddy's pretty face looked serious. "I wish —"

"What do you wish, Toddy?"

"Oh, nothing," she said, giving her head a little toss. "Now it's your turn to ask me something you don't know about me."

"Did you read the Class Prophecy?" Dan asked.

"Of course, why?"

"Well, was it true? Are you going to become a famous actress?"

For a minute Toddy looked startled, then she seemed to shudder slightly. "Oh, no!"

"But you won the Drama Prize at the Awards Banquet for playing Portia in *The Merchant of Venice.*"

"Well, that's all it was, playing — I want to do something much more worthwhile than *that!*" she declared.

A whistle blew. "Time's up!" shouted Mr. Dean. "Did you get to know one of your classmates better?" A loud "Yeah!" came forth. "Good!" the coach beamed. "Now, we're going to have some music. Enjoy the rest of the evening!"

Chris came to claim Toddy for the first dance. Dan went in search of Laurel, only to find to his chagrin that she had already been wisked onto the dance floor.

Not wanting to dance with anyone else, Dan was forced to stand on the sidelines, watching until the set was over. When the third dance ended, he began weaving his way through the dancers over to her when another announcement was made.

"Ladies and gentlemen, the next dance is

a 'Paul Jones.' Ladies make a circle and gentlemen form a circle around them, moving counterclockwise to the music. When it stops, whoever you're standing opposite is your partner for the next set."

"Come on, let's get into the circle!" said Toddy, grabbing both Laurel's and Kit's hands.

The music started and the two circles began to move. Some of the guys, trying to guess when the band was going to stop playing and wanting to be opposite a favorite partner, would either quicken or slow their pace accordingly. Laurel saw that Dan was one of those. He was trying to keep his eye on her position. But when the music finally stopped, he was standing right in front of Kit.

Amused, Laurel glanced at her friend, then caught her breath. She had never realized before how beautiful Kit was. There was both delicacy and strength in her fine features. Her luminous gray eyes lighted up and a smile trembled on her sweetly curved mouth as she held out her hand to Dan.

For a moment Kit's face was unmasked. And then Laurel saw something more, something she wasn't intended to see. Kit was in love with Dan!

13

Then summer was over. The maple trees along the street began turning gold. The Virginia creeper clinging to the sides of the house blushed crimson. In the mornings, thin frost glistened on the lawn and mist rose, blurring the sharpness of the blue line of hills surrounding Meadowridge.

Soon, like leaves scattering in the wind, everyone would be going away, each to a different destination, a whole new life — Toddy to Europe with Helene and Mrs. Hale; Kit, for her first year at Merrivale College. Chris Blanchard had already left for the University and Dan had gone off to college. Only Laurel was left behind.

Returning home one September afternoon and hearing in the distance a train whistle at the Meadowridge crossing, Laurel paused to listen. It had such a melancholy sound, as wistful as her own thoughts.

She sighed, unlatched the gate, and walked up the path and into the house. For the first time the place was depressing. The home that had always seemed so warm and welcoming now seemed somehow cold and hostile. In just a little over a week, everything had changed — ever since she had brought up the subject of going away to a Music Conservatory to continue her vocal studies.

Laurel had avoided Mr. Fordyce all summer, hoping not to run into him on the street or at church, afraid he would press her for a decision. Realizing she had been putting it off, and apprehensive of the outcome, she had gathered her courage and first broached it with Papa Lee. She had gone around to his office at the back of the house early one morning before any patients were due.

She recalled every detail of that scene now with a little shudder.

"Dismiss it from your mind" had been Dr. Woodward's first shocked reaction. "A young lady your age traveling across the country by herself? It's out of the question."

Laurel bit her tongue, ready to remind him that she had taken that same long trip years ago as a child. She had carefully rehearsed all the reasons he ought to give her permission to go, backing them up with Mr.

Fordyce's supportive comments. She thought she had met every objection he might raise, but she had not been prepared for this unexpectedly abrupt refusal.

In a voice that shook she pleaded, "Will you at least think about it, Papa Lee, discuss it with Mother?"

"Discuss what with me?" a voice behind her asked, and Laurel turned to see Ava standing in the office doorway, her arms filled with purple asters she was bringing from her garden for Leland's waiting room.

The scene that followed was worse than Laurel could have imagined. Ava's reaction was immediate and volatile. Her face turned pale, her eyes dark and wild with alarm.

"But you can't possibly go so far and alone! No, I won't hear of it!" she protested. "Leland, talk to her!"

Laurel looked helplessly at Dr. Woodward. The face that had always beheld her with such indulgent love was now grave, the eyes usually twinkling with affection and fondness now seemed unfathomable.

"But, Mother, *you* were the one who wanted me to study voice in the first place. It was *you* who said I had a gift I should develop. I would never have even thought of it if you hadn't encouraged me, had Mr. Fordyce give me lessons —" Laurel turned a bewildered gaze on Ava.

"But I never dreamed it would take you away from me — from *us!*" she said indignantly. Then changing her tactics, she added, "I still believe you have a gift and I want you to go on with your lessons, of course."

"But Mr. Fordyce says he's taught me all he can. He says I *need* further training elsewhere — at a Music Conservatory — if I'm to learn what I must learn —"

"To do what? To become a professional singer? To go on the stage?" Ava flung out her hands in a helpless gesture. "I never heard of such nonsense. What is Milton Fordyce thinking of to put such ideas into a young girl's head?"

"Papa —" Laurel began, but Dr. Woodward held up his hand warningly.

"I don't think we should discuss this further right now. I have patients coming in a few minutes and we all need to calm down," he said soothingly. "Ava, my dear, there is no use upsetting yourself. Nothing will be decided or settled right away. When we are all more composed, we can talk about this reasonably."

But they had not talked it over calmly or reasonably. They had not talked it over at all. Laurel waited for one of them to reopen the discussion, but nothing was ever said. It was as though the whole subject had never been mentioned.

Everything went on as before, and yet everything had changed subtly. Laurel felt both of them watching her, not angrily but with disappointment and bewilderment. She sensed they felt they had somehow failed to make her happy since she wanted to leave them.

In turn, she felt guilty and ashamed, knowing they must think her unappreciative, ungrateful. Ava's face became strained. A sad, anxious expression gave it a pinched look. Laurel struggled with her conscience. Her deep desire had always been to please, but something new began to assert itself. Did she not have a right to explore the person she was apart from these dear adoptive parents? And if they had not believed in her talent why had they encouraged her? It was all so dismaying and disturbing.

Dreams do not die easily, however, and Mr. Fordyce had fueled Laurel's hope. The memory of Kit's graduation speech strengthened her. "To thine own self be true." Laurel must be true to herself, she thought. She could not continue living the safe, sheltered life others wanted for her. Her own true identity demanded to be free. Whether that would be through her voice or whatever might be waiting for her in Boston, she knew she must pursue it.

She was torn between loyalty to her secret goal and loving sympathy for the Woodwards, and decided not to spoil the holidays by bringing up the subject of leaving until after the New Year.

So Laurel plunged herself into the church choir's Christmas performance of Handel's *Messiah*, so that much of her time was taken up by rehearsals. Willingly taking on Ava's Christmas list, she kept herself busy with shopping and wrapping presents. In the kitchen she helped Ella and Jenny with the holiday baking.

Sometimes she felt like a puppet, with someone else pulling the strings, making her move and get up in the morning. Too often there were purple shadows of sleeplessness under her eyes, their lids swollen by tears shed at night. What was to become of her? she daily asked herself. Was she wrong? Was leaving selfish? Desperately Laurel prayed for guidance: "Show me Thy way, Lord, that I might find favor with Thee."

Dan wrote he could not come home for Christmas; he couldn't afford the train fare. Lost in her own dilemma, the uncertainty about her future, Dan seemed very far away.

The days before Christmas seemed outwardly serene, peaceful, but within Laurel, a fire storm raged.

The performance of the *Messiah* was hailed by everyone who attended as the finest program Meadowridge Community Church choir had ever presented. Afterwards there was a reception in the festively decorated social hall. It was the custom to hang small gilt-paper cornucopias on the church Christmas tree. Inside each cornucopia was a slip of paper bearing a Scripture verse. These were considered each person's special Bible message for the coming year.

When Laurel opened hers, she read: "Be strong and of good courage; be not afraid, neither be thou dismayed; for the Lord, thy God is with thee whithersoever thou goest" (Joshua 1:9). It seemed a confirmation, and Laurel took it as such. Her conviction grew that she *must* go.

The New Year came and a week later Laurel gathered up her courage and went into Dr. Woodward's office. The sun was streaming in through the windows of the small L-shaped office, a fire going in the Franklin stove took the chill off the January morning. Its warmth accentuated the combined smells of old leather from the shelves of medical books, the Jonathan apples in the bowl he kept on his desk to reward small pa-

151

tients, and the spicy pine scent of the crackling wood.

At Laurel's entrance, Dr. Woodward looked up with pleasure, but that look slowly faded into alarm as she stammered out her reason for coming.

In a voice that shook slightly Laurel told him she had written the Music Conservatory in Boston for an application, and that Mr. Fordyce had given her names of a few well-known teachers she could contact and now she was determined to go.

He took a long time responding. He turned and gazed out the window for an interminable minute, his hands under his chin, his fingers pressed together forming an arch. When he looked back around at Laurel, his eyes were full of concern.

"Do you have any idea what this will do to your mother?" he asked solemnly.

Laurel felt her heart accelerate frantically. Steeling herself for the attack on her emotions that would follow, Laurel begged, "Papa Lee, I *have* to go. Please don't make it any harder than it's going to be!"

But it had been hard, the hardest thing Laurel had ever done in her life. The last thing she had ever wanted to do was hurt these two dear people.

When all possible arguments against her

going failed, the Woodwards retreated into injured silence. Laurel hardened her heart self-protectively, knowing if she did not she would be trapped by pity. Even if she came back, she had to go now. Didn't they see that?

The night before her departure, while packing in her bedroom, she heard Ava's muffled sobs. Overcome with compassion, she almost ran down the hall to her adoptive mother's room. She wished there were some way to comfort her. But she knew the only comfort Ava would accept would be compliance. Knowing she could not give that, Laurel put her face in her hands and wept.

She had meant to bring only happiness to these two who had given her so much. Instead, she was causing them grief and distress.

Morning came at last. A gray, wet mist cloaked the barren trees outside her bedroom window. Her train departed at seven. She knew Ava would not come down to say goodbye, or see her off. Laurel dressed and carried her suitcase and small valise downstairs. She stood in the front hall, straining to hear some movement upstairs that might indicate that either Ava or Dr. Woodward were up, that perhaps they might relent and give her their blessing before she left.

Laurel stood in front of the hall mirror, as she had so many other happier times, to put on her hat. As she did, she saw an envelope propped against the vase. In Dr. Woodward's bold scribble was her name. She picked it up and opened it. Inside were five crisp twenty-dollar bills and two fifty-dollar bills. But there was no note.

Laurel pressed her lips together tightly. The night before, he had kissed her cheek and said "Good night, my dear" as usual. At least there had been no last-minute request that she change her mind. Ava had nursed a migraine in her room all day. It was no more than Laurel expected.

Her heart was heavy with all that was unspoken between them.

A minute later she saw Jenny's reflection in the mirror behind her as she came from the kitchen and stood in the archway of the dining room.

Slowly Laurel turned around. Jenny sniffed and wiped her eyes with a balled handkerchief. Laurel felt a rush of affection for Jenny, who had been her confidante, her comforter, her exhorter, her friend. Spontaneously the hired girl opened her arms and Laurel went into them. She could feel Jenny's shoulders shaking with suppressed sobs.

"I'll be back. Don't cry!" Laurel whispered, patting her.

"Your cab's out front." Jenny sniffled,

pushing Laurel away gently. Her plump chin was trembling as she looked at her with red-rimmed eyes and in spite of her brimming tears, nodded approvingly. "I must say, you do look very smart and grown up, Laurel."

Laurel walked over to the foot of the stairway and stood there a minute, looking up. Should she go back upstairs, knock at Mother's door, say all the things that were in her heart to say? She glanced over at Jenny who met the look with a sorrowful shake of her head.

Laurel sighed. Jenny was right. It would just make things worse. She picked up her coat, put it on, straightened the brim of her hat. Walking resolutely to the front door, she blew Jenny a kiss, picked up her bags, and went out into the mist-veiled morning.

She closed the door behind her and its click took on symbolic significance. She knew she was leaving something precious and yet something from which she had to flee, or it might cripple her forever.

At the station, Laurel waited impatiently. Now that she had come this far, she wanted no further delay. She was tense with apprehension, the nervous anticipation of all that lay ahead.

The platform was deserted. Laurel saw no one she knew. No other passengers from

Meadowridge seemed to be boarding the early train. Except for the clerk in the office, no one was around.

Finally the train rounded the bend and came to a stop with the screech of steel brakes on the rails, steam hissing from its engine. No one else boarded, and only mailbags were exchanged from one of the boxcars farther down the line.

The whistle blew shrilly. Heart pounding, Laurel moved toward the train. At the entrance to the coach, she turned to take a last look around. She remembered the first time she had seen the rolling Meadowridge hills when she had stepped off the Orphan Train onto this same platform years before. When would she see it all again?

"All aboard, miss," the conductor said, coming up beside her and offering his hand to assist her up the high steps into the train.

Entering the car, she saw it was nearly empty except for a few sleeping passengers. She found an unoccupied seat and put her valise in the rack above, then sat down on the scratchy red upholstery. She was taking off her hat when she heard the chug of the engine and felt the train begin to move. As it lurched forward, Laurel pressed her face against the window, looking back to watch until the yellow station house was out of sight.

14

Boston! She was here at last! Laurel thought to herself peering eagerly out the window of the hired hack. She had followed Mr. Fordyce's instructions to take one from the train station and go straight to the rooming house near the Music Conservatory.

Until now Boston had been only a name in a history book. A name associated with the Boston Tea Party and the poem she had memorized in school about Paul Revere's ride to Lexington to warn of the British coming. Now, here she was in the heart of the great historic city called "the Hub of the Universe" and "the Cradle of Liberty."

As she looked first to the right and then to the left, she was filled with excitement. The city was alive with people and activities, a long distance from Meadowridge's sleepy, small-town atmosphere. It bustled with noise and movement. Here things happened, here anything seemed possible.

Of course, she could not remember much about Boston from the days she had lived here with her mother as a little girl. Children are only aware of their immediate surroundings, and Laurel's memories of that time were centered on her life with Mama in the cozy upstairs flat of Mrs. Campbell's house.

The streets were winding and rather narrow, lined with tall brick buildings of imposing architecture. The heart of the city was a jumble of businesses, banks and churches. Trolleys sped right down the middle of the street, vying for space with wagons loaded with produce and elegant buggies. And right in the center was a huge park where people strolled and children played.

Laurel had given the cab driver the address of the rooming house run by a distant relative of a former college classmate of Mr. Fordyce.

"I'm sure it's not luxurious, but it's clean, comfortable, and conveniently near the Conservatory," he had told her. "The rates are very reasonable and that's important since there are always unforeseen expenses once you're a student, and everything adds up."

Everything he had told her about the boardinghouse was true. What Mr. Fordyce hadn't told Laurel, she soon found out for herself. Mrs. Sombey, the landlady, was insatiably curious. Laurel felt she was being interviewed for a position instead of renting a room, and only managed to escape by saying she had to go right over to the Music Conservatory. Eager to begin her adventure, she covered the few short blocks quickly.

Laurel's heart sounded like a percussion instrument to her as she stood looking up at the Music Conservatory building. Her first instinct was to turn and run. How dare she think herself ready to brave such a prestigious institution, present herself as a candidate for admission as a student here?

Well, she had come this far and she was not going to turn back now. She reminded herself of all that her decision had cost her emotionally, to say nothing of the Woodwards. Fortifying herself with her own version of the Scripture verse that speaks of setting one's "hand to the plow," Laurel started up the stone steps and opened the door into the entrance lobby.

Once inside, a cacophony of sounds greeted her ears. Assorted music floated through the transoms of a dozen practice rooms, merging into an unplanned symphony. Woodwinds, violins, cellos, piano and French horns, all blended in an exciting, if not perfectly harmonic, whole. From somewhere she heard a soprano vocalizing the scales and echoing down the hall came an a cappella chorus of male and female voices.

Proceeding timidly, Laurel followed a sign with an arrow directing her to the Administration Office. In a burst of laughter a group of chattering young people, carrying portfolios and music sheets, came rushing down the main steps. Laurel moved against the wall to let them go by, thinking soon she would be one of them. A thrill of nervous excitement rippled through Laurel. She *was* actually here! Here, where others like herself had come to take that step into serious musical training.

Mr. Fordyce's oft-repeated admonition to all his students rang in her ears as clearly as the sound of a flute being practiced in one of the rooms: "A career in music is one of the most difficult professions in which to achieve success. It takes more than talent and interest. To attain even a minimum, one must be absolutely dedicated, be convinced that music is the most important thing in life."

Laurel felt something tighten within her. Was that *her* feeling about music? To be truthful, she knew it was only means to an end. But she would honestly try not to waste this opportunity. If she were accepted, she would do her best. That she could promise.

An hour later Laurel's initial excitement had drained away. She held in her hand a sheaf of forms that must be completed before she could apply for her first interview for admission to the Conservatory. Telling herself she was just tired from the long train trip and that things would look brighter once she was settled, she went back to the rooming house and unpacked. At least, she was here in Boston, her plans underway. It would all work out, Laurel assured herself. But a week later she encountered a more discouraging setback.

At the Music Conservatory, Laurel was shocked to find that she would have to audition before she could qualify for admission, and the audition list was long. Perhaps she should have applied long before leaving Meadowridge to insure a place on the list for next fall's classes. After applying for an audition, she would be given a date and time to appear before a board of the faculty. Then it was a matter of waiting to find out if she was accepted as a student.

Laurel's heart sank. She had never imagined it would be so difficult. She was sure even Mr. Fordyce was not aware it would take this long. In the meantime, what was she to do?

As Laurel left the Admissions Office, she encountered another young woman checking the bulletin board on which the audition list was posted.

"I know just how you feel," the girl said. "I applied the first time last spring. If you have a coach — preferably, one of the teachers here — your chances are better."

"A coach?"

"Yes, someone to keep you on your mark so that when you do get to audition, you're at peak."

"But, I don't know anyone —" Laurel began, feeling even more discouraged. "How does one find a coach?"

"Well, I was lucky that my violin teacher is a recognized coach. Do you live in Boston?"

"I just came. I mean, I've only been here a short time."

The girl frowned. "You mean you don't know anyone locally who could help you?"

Laurel shook her head.

"Then I'd advise you to check at the office. They should have a list of teachers willing to coach." The girl made a wry face.

162

"It's expensive though. They charge by the hour and they want their money first. You know how it is with musicians, always broke! But it's worth it . . . at least, I *hope* it's worth it."

With that, the girl picked up her violin case, wished her luck, and left. Laurel stared at the long list of names and scheduled audition dates. It was discouraging but not hopeless, Laurel told herself.

Following the advice the other student had given her, Laurel checked at the office for a list of coaches. Everything the girl had said was confirmed. The list of available coaches was much shorter than the list of hopeful applicants for auditions, the hourly price of lessons daunting.

Downhearted, Laurel left the cavernous hall outside the administration office, pushed open the door to go out of the building, and found it was raining very hard outside.

One thing she had learned since arriving in Boston midwinter was that the weather was as uncertain as her future now looked. Luckily she had taken an umbrella with her when she started out that morning.

Buttoning the top of her coat, she shifted her music portfolio more securely under one arm, then opened her umbrella and, using it as a shield against the driving rain, she started down the steps.

Preoccupied with her new set of problems and trying to hold the umbrella steady against the gusty wind, Laurel did not see the figure hurrying up the Conservatory steps heading directly toward her until their two umbrellas collided with a jarring thrust, halting them both.

"Oh, sorry!" a male voice said just as Laurel exclaimed, "Excuse me!"

As she righted her umbrella, Laurel saw a tall, young man in a caped coat, also carrying a portfolio. For a moment they inspected each other. Then he lowered his umbrella to tip his hat. At that moment the wind whipped the hat out of his hand and sent it whirling down the steps, depositing it in a puddle at the bottom of the steps.

"Oh, my!" cried Laurel in dismay.

But the young man only laughed. As he started after it, he called back over his shoulder, "No problem!"

Laurel hurried to the bottom of the steps, where he was retrieving the hat, shaking the water from its brim.

"I'm dreadfully sorry. I wasn't looking where I was going!" Laurel apologized. "Is it ruined?"

"No harm done," he assured her. "It will

164

dry out." He replaced the top hat at a rakish angle and grinned. "Beastly day, isn't it?"

What an attractive man! Hatless, his thick hair had sprung into a tangle of dark curls, Laurel observed. His eyes, too, were dark and crinkled in the corners, as if he found much to laugh about. How wonderful to take life as it came, she thought, the mishaps as well as the lucky moments.

"Well, I must be off, or I'll be late!" he said and went bounding up the steps and into the building.

Laurel stood there a minute longer, staring after him. His easy laughter reminded her of Toddy, who had always helped her see the bright side. She suddenly missed her old friends more than ever. Both Toddy and Kit had always been there for her when things went wrong. And things seemed to be going very wrong for her right now.

Sighing, she moved on in the direction of her boardinghouse. Maybe she should have reported to the Conservatory the minute she arrived, found out about the possible delay of enrolling as a student. But there was something Laurel had wanted to do first.

Finding Mrs. Campbell's house had been a priority. Mama had made Laurel memorize her address in the unlikely event she should ever get lost, and Laurel had never forgotten it. But when she got there, she discovered that the whole row of old frame houses on the street she remembered had been destroyed by fire several years before, and a warehouse had been erected in their place.

The neighborhood itself looked run-down, not at all as she remembered it. Of course, she had only been a child then, and it was possible that nostalgia had distorted the facts.

Although this was a disappointing set-back, her hoped-for source of information gone, Laurel was still determined to pursue her search for her real family.

All this had meant countless, time-consuming hours, and long, usually fruitless excursions. The days of February, spent in the musty archives of the courthouse slipped away. Here, Laurel had pored over old records, checking out hunches and hints that led nowhere.

Finally one day in the County Records office, much to her joy, Laurel found the marriage license issued to Lillian Maynard of Back Bay, and Paul Vestal. Shortly afterward she also found her father's death recorded, though no place of burial was given.

And Laurel made the rounds of several cemeteries, looking for his grave, all to no avail.

But the most traumatic trip of all was the one she took out to Greystone Orphanage. She went by trolley, having to transfer twice, then walked up a long steep hill. Her heart was pounding, not so much from the climb, but from remembered apprehension, reliving that awful morning when she and her mama had come there together. It was the last time she had ever seen her mother.

The large stone building stood like a fortress, the chain-link fence surrounding it every bit as prison like and forbidding as she remembered. She had thought she could go in, make some inquiries, and see if she could gain any more information that might help her in her search. But the emotions that assailed her were too overwhelming. Laurel had turned around, practically run back down the hill and caught the next trolley that came along. The experience was too shattering to repeat, and she had never gone back.

Now Laurel suspected she had wasted valuable time that might have been better spent establishing herself as a student at the Music Conservatory. Her name had been placed on a long list of applicants, but her audition date was still weeks away. And she had learned that, in addition to giving a successful audition, one was required to supply three professional recommendations. Even with all that, there was no guarantee of acceptance.

Laurel's spirits were at a new low when she wrote to Mr. Fordyce, explaining her dilemma and asking him not to mention this latest delay to her parents. So far she received no reply.

But what could he do, after all? She had no other professional connections. Where had she sung except at church and school? And no one in the big city of Boston had ever heard of Meadowridge!

15

March blew into Boston like the proverbial lion, blustery days of cold rain which more often than not turned into sleet, coating streets and sidewalks with hazardous ice.

On one particular morning, the wind off the river was knife sharp as Laurel cut across the Common, her head bent, her umbrella slanted against the stinging rain. She had gone to the Conservatory to check the auditions list, in case her name had moved any further up. Of course, it had not. Neither had she heard from Mr. Fordyce yet. Perhaps she should see about getting a coach. That, of course, meant spending money. She had been holding onto her cash reserve, but now she wondered if she should not make that investment. Oh, there was so very much to think about, to decide.

Laurel had never dreamed living on her

own in the city would be so expensive. The money Dr. Woodward gave her before she left Meadowridge seemed more than adequate, but everything cost so much more here than she had imagined. She knew she would have to find work soon or — or what? Laurel did not even want to contemplate what might happen when her money ran out.

The thought of returning to her small room at the boarding house on this dreary day was too depressing. There she would have nothing to think about but her troubles. Besides, she was suddenly very hungry, so she headed for the small restaurant on the corner where she could get some lunch.

Pushing open the door of the restaurant, Laurel immediately felt its warmth enfold her. The delicious fragrance of freshly baked bread and the aroma of newly brewed coffee tickled her nostrils with their promise of satisfaction. A bowl of the thick vegetable soup made here daily and a slice of the crusty bread would revive her energy and her spirits.

She gave the pretty, dark-eyed waitress her order, then looked out the window. Laurel always chose a table by the wall near a window if it was available because she liked looking out on the busy street. It made her feel less lonely to watch other people, make up stories about them, where they were going, where they had been.

This was a game she had begun playing since she had moved here. After living in Meadowridge where she knew almost everyone and everyone knew her, it was a strange sensation to be alone in a city the size of Boston, where no one ever called you by name. Homesickness was a battle Laurel fought daily. Although she had only been here a few weeks, they had been the longest weeks of her life.

That's why she liked this cheerful little place with its friendly atmosphere. It was still early for the usual lunch crowd. Laurel enjoyed seeing the easy camaraderie between the staff and the customers, even though she was too shy to be a part of it.

As she sat there staring at passers-by, Laurel wondered what she could do to earn some money to stretch her small amount of cash beyond her rent and bare necessities. The first and most natural thought was to give piano lessons to children. But, in a city filled with aspiring musicians all in need of extra money to pay for their tuition and extra coaching, would there be an excess of them offering music lessons?

Refusing to be defeated before she even

tried, Laurel decided she would place an ad in the newspaper. She would state her willingness to give lessons at pupils' own homes, both piano and voice.

All at once, the irony of her situation struck her. How similar to her mother's! Here in this same place, Boston, Lillian Vestal, too, had been forced to find work as a music teacher in order to support herself and her small child.

Laurel's memories of her mother were priceless, kept locked in her heart all these years like precious jewels. Now, she felt free to take them out, handling them delicately, examining, marveling and appreciating the magical childhood she had been given, even in the direst of circumstances.

She cherished the memory of being held in loving arms, of the pretty face above her framed in a cloud of dark hair, of the low, sweet voice singing her to sleep. At Greystone those memories had devastated her and yet, at the same time, sustained her. Then she had pretended their separation was only temporary, that soon they would be reunited. Even after she went on the "Orphan Train" to Meadowridge and was adopted by the Woodwards, her "real" mother had remained a phantom presence in Laurel's life.

Thinking about her, Laurel looked out the restaurant window into the rain-swept street, trying to bring that face into clear focus. But it was another one that superimposed itself on the vague image. It was Ava Woodward's face Laurel saw. Her face as she had last seen it — drawn, white, with alarming purple shadows ringing her eyes. The memory struck her conscience. She could hardly bear to think of Ava or of Dr. Lee. But if she had broken their hearts, her heart was breaking, too.

"Here we are, miss," announced the waitress in a cheerful tone.

Laurel turned away from the window as the steaming bowl of soup was set before her, and Ava's reproachful image disappeared.

Laurel ate, gradually feeling revived and more hopeful. Surely things must get better.

"Will there by anything else, miss?" the waitress asked. "For dessert today, we've got a lovely caramel custard and there's apple cobbler just out of the oven."

Laurel's mouth watered at the suggestion, but until she had a job she had to be careful, so she shook her head regretfully.

"No thanks, this will be plenty," she said, visions of Ella's delectable pies and cakes flashing tauntingly through her mind.

Just at that moment the door of the restaurant burst open and, with a gust of wind and rain, a young man dashed inside, closing his umbrella with a flourish as well as a great showering of water onto nearby patrons.

"Oh, sorry! I do beg your pardon!" he said in a deep, rich voice, bestowing an absolutely irresistible smile upon his victims.

His entrance in so small a place could not go unnoticed and Laurel, with the other customers, turned her head to look at the arrival. To her amazement, it was the same young man she had collided with on the steps of the Conservatory a few weeks before.

Mr. Pasquini, the restaurant owner, came hurrying forward, greeting him with the enthusiasm one reserved for a long-lost relative or visiting celebrity.

"Welcome, welcome! How went the tour?"

"Bravissimo!" replied the young man, divesting himself of his coat and hanging it on the wooden cloak-tree near the door. "It was better than we expected. Sold out crowds every night. But I missed your wonderful pasta . . . and no one can make bread like Maria!" He kissed the tips of his fingers in an extravagant gesture of praise.

"Well, come along, sit, sit! First some minestrone, yes? Then, some linguini, maybe?"

The young man rubbed his hands together in evident anticipation.

"Fine, fine!" Smiling, he looked around, and quite suddenly he met Laurel's gaze.

Aware that she had been staring, fascinated, she flushed and averted her eyes, looking down into her empty soup bowl. For some reason her heart was giving quick little leaps.

Her first impression of the young man was reaffirmed. He was extremely handsome. This time she noticed his teeth — very white against olive skin. Possibly he was of Italian descent, he seemed so at home here. There were quite a few Italian people living in the vicinity of her boardinghouse and the Music Conservatory.

Mr. Pasquini had mentioned a "tour." Did that mean the young man was a professional musician returning from a successful road tour? That day they had bumped into each other so unceremoniously on the steps of the Conservatory, Laurel had assumed he was a student. Although her curiosity about him was piqued, she had learned nothing more.

Having finished her lunch, she could not

continue to occupy a table without ordering something more. Since it was near noon, the restaurant was beginning to fill up as all the "regulars" were arriving.

Reluctantly Laurel put on her coat and, taking her check, went up to the cash register to pay. There she noticed Mr. Pasquini hovering at the table of the young man, engaging him in lively conversation. Laurel got her change and with no further reason to linger, went out again into the stormy March day.

It seemed an odd sort of coincidence to see that young man again, Laurel thought, as she struggled to raise her umbrella. In this big city she rarely saw anyone twice. It was a city of strangers where she, too, was a stranger.

Her decision to advertise for piano pupils in the newspaper now settled, she knew she must get a newspaper to see how such ads were worded and how much it would cost. There was a newsstand on the corner about a block from where she lived. Braving the wind, she decided to walk to save carfare and by the time she reached the newsstand the hem of her coat and dress were quite soaked and she could feel the damp seeping in through her thin leather shoes.

Miserable and shivering, she hurried

along the slick sidewalks, being splashed by the horses and carriages that went by the busy thoroughfare. For some reason she thought of her father who had been run over and killed on just such a stormy day in this very same city. Her father was still such a shadowy figure in her life. Laurel had no real memory of him, although she was two when he died. All she had was the picture in the locket.

When she had first come to Boston, Laurel had made the rounds of galleries and art dealers' shops, hoping that by chance, she might someday find one of her father's paintings.

But after she learned Mrs. Campbell's house had been razed by fire, she assumed they had probably all burned in the attic where they were stored.

Chilled to the bone, Laurel reached the boardinghouse and mounted the narrow stairway to her second-floor room. Longingly she thought of Ella's cozy kitchen where she had come in from school on many a rainy day to find hot chocolate or spicy tea waiting, and homemade cookies, still warm from the oven.

Quickly she got out of her wet things and curled up at the end of the bed, spreading the newspaper out in front of her. As she turned over the rain-dampened pages, going toward the classified section, something caught her eye, an item in the society news.

"Mrs. Bennett Maynard will be the hostess of a soiree next Tuesday evening to benefit the Symphony —"

The name seemed to leap at Laurel from the page. She noted the address — in the most exclusive residential section of the city. The brief article gave only the most discreet information: "Symphony supporters, only those holding season tickets, are invited to call between the hours of four and six. The Symphony's Music Director will speak on the selection of next year's program and possible guest artists to be featured in future performances."

Could *this* Mrs. Maynard be her grandmother?

Laurel determined that the next day she would take the trolley out to that part of town and look for the house matching the address given. Maybe, at last she would see the place that belonged to her mother's family, the house where Lillian Maynard had grown up and left to marry Paul Vestal.

Laurel was pretty well convinced now that her young parents had eloped. Why else the estrangement? A girl from Boston's Back

Bay, with breeding and background, marry a penniless artist? Why, such an alliance would have been considered unthinkable in an earlier day. Yet the young couple was so madly in love, Laurel romanticized, that perhaps they knew there was no other way to be together. And in running away they had irrevocably broken all their ties. Yes, she would go and see. Maybe even to-morrow, Laurel decided.

But the next morning she awakened with a sore throat and fever and the next two weeks she was laid up with a heavy cold and laryngitis. When she finally made it shakily out of bed and went over to the Conservatory, she found to her despair that she had missed her scheduled audition date.

16

Laurel's disappointment over the missed audition was combined with unexpected relief. Maybe she really wasn't ready. It would be far worse to try and fail. After all, she could not be blamed for having a bad cold. But, if, unprepared and uncoached, she was rejected, that would be her fault.

What she had heard about the auditions was confusing. She did not know how the decision was made. Did the board base a student's acceptance on the difficulty of the piece or on the clarity of vocalization, on poise and stage presence or on one's presentation with integrity to the composer? Laurel had no idea.

Perhaps missing her audition was all for the best. Before the next auditions were scheduled, she would have time to find a coach to help her. But a coach cost money.

That meant she must find a way to supplement her income.

Ever since her arrival in Boston, Laurel had received a small check from Dr. Woodward at the first of each month. Because of the circumstances under which she had left Meadowridge, however, she felt guilty using his money and so far she had resisted cashing any of the checks. But unless she found some way of earning some soon, she would be forced to do so.

To Laurel's delight the ad she had placed in the newspaper brought immediate response from many of Boston's socially active mothers. With their children industriously occupied at the piano at home, these ladies were free to be about their visiting or shopping or having tea with friends, a very convenient arrangement.

Laurel's first pleasure in receiving so many responses to her ad was soon diminished somewhat when she realized that teaching music in her pupils' homes meant hours of her time spent on trolleys, trams and on foot to reach the various addresses.

Neither had she imagined teaching to be so tedious. Listening over and over to clumsy little fingers stumbling over scales, or distorting such simple tunes as "Welcome, Sweet Springtime" sometimes made her feel like screaming. But her determination to be independent was more important than the boredom and weariness. It was a price she was more than willing to pay. Saving money for a coach meant practicing many small economies.

Her first resolution was that of eating only one full meal a day. It took some ingenuity for her to smuggle fruit and crackers, concealed in her music bag, past her eagle-eyed landlady, and make tea on a small spirit-burner bought in a second-hand store. For her one meal Laurel continued to frequent the restaurant on the corner, a few blocks from her rooming house.

After a short spring Laurel discovered Boston's summers were as extreme as its winters. Hot and humid days were followed by breathless nights when the air barely stirred the curtains of her bedroom windows. To make matters worse, several of her pupils canceled their lessons to vacation with their families at second homes on the coast of Maine or Cape Cod, where Boston's affluent spent their summers.

The unaccustomed heat and the prospect of the loss of extra income upon which she had come to rely were depressing, and Laurel struggled not to succumb to feelings of loneliness and self-doubt. She had to keep reminding herself of her main purpose in coming east.

With less traveling and teaching to take up her day, Laurel had more time to think about contacting Mrs. Bennett Maynard whom she had come to believe was her grandmother. She often took out that newspaper article and reread it. If this *really* was her Mama's mother, how did she go about approaching her? Since the woman must be advancing in years by now, it wouldn't do to show up on her doorstep, announcing herself. The encounter must be arranged with careful thought and tact.

One Saturday, Laurel decided to go out to the address given and see for herself what might have been her mother's childhood home. She took a trolley to the end of the line, then at the direction of the conductor, walked another few blocks. She strolled along quiet streets, lined with impressive homes set well back from the boulevard over which arched tall, shady elms.

Laurel walked slowly, looking for the house number in the clipping she held in her hand. Then, all at once she saw it! Displayed discreetly on a polished brass plaque set among climbing ivy in the post of a brick wall was the house number she was looking for.

Number 1573 was a stately pink brick of Federal architecture, its many windows covered with black louvered shutters. Curved double steps with ornamental black iron railings led up to a paneled front door flanked by tubs of espaliered trees.

There was no sign of life, not on the street itself, nor in the house. No movement at all behind those shuttered windows. Did Mama's family go to Maine or Martha's Vineyard, in the summer?

For a long time, Laurel stood looking at the house, then slowly turned and retraced her steps. She was hardly conscious when she left the luxurious serenity of that part of town inhabited by the city's wealthy and prestigious citizens and boarded the trolley to return to the workaday life of the rest of the population of Boston.

Laurel got off at her usual stop, still distracted by her pilgrimage, walked over two blocks to the little restaurant where she took her evening meal. Entering, she was glad to see her favorite small table in the corner vacant. Seating herself, she picked up the menu, looking at it without actually reading it.

Her thoughts were filled with the significance of her afternoon excursion. The grandeur of those mansions, guarded by ornamental iron fences or well-trimmed boxwood hedges, their manicured terraces and shuttered windows had cast a strange spell on Laurel. She tried to imagine the beautiful girl of her locket, with her laughing eyes and flowing dark hair, her dainty figure and exquisite clothes, who had lived in one of them and who had become her mother.

Now she began to see Mrs. Campbell's flat in all its shabbiness through the eyes of one once accustomed to luxury and comfort. She saw the shiny black of her mother's one coat with its worn fur collar and cuffs. The rare treats of cake or fruit to celebrate small occasions must have been eked out of a meager income. Yet Laurel had never heard her mother complain — not even when her living conditions brought about the illness that caused her death!

Laurel's thoughts were interrupted by a rich, male voice. "I recommend the lasagna tonight."

Laurel started and looked up at the waiter. She fumbled with the menu as she recognized him as no other than the young man with whom she had collided on one of her first times at the Conservatory. The very same one whom she had seen later right here in this restaurant.

Surprised speechless, Laurel simply stared at him. His smile widened and he said, "To answer your question. Yes, I am a student at the Conservatory, and I work here part-time to support myself *and* my voice coach!"

Laurel felt her face flame with embarrassment.

"Oh, well, I —" she stammered. "I'm sorry, I didn't —"

"Don't apologize, please! We all — at least most of us — have to work while we attend the Conservatory. It goes with the territory, as they say. Surely there is no such thing as an artist of any kind who doesn't have to struggle, is there? If so, I haven't heard of one, much less met one." His dark eyes sparkled with amusement. "Now, what about you? I mean, what would you like for dinner?"

Flustered, Laurel looked down at the menu, none of the selections making sense. It was usually her pocketbook that dictated her order anyway.

"May I make a suggestion?" he continued. "I've personally sampled the minestrone soup and found it to be, as usual, delicious. But then, perhaps, it's too warm an evening for soup. Maybe something lighter. The lasagna is delicious and, with a fresh green salad, perfect." He paused. "Even though we both know we have encountered each other before, may I introduce myself formally?" He gave a small bow. "I'm Gene Michela."

It would have seemed rude not to do the same. "I'm Laurel Vestal."

"Am I correct in assuming you are also a student at the Conservatory?"

"Well, not exactly. At least, not yet. That is, I haven't been accepted. I missed my audition and — I found out I should have a coach — So I've been teaching, giving piano lessons. I had ten pupils but now most of them are away for the summer and I —" Suddenly she halted, blushing. Why on earth was she talking so much, telling all this to a — a *waiter?*

But he was regarding her sympathetically, nodding with understanding.

"Oh, dear!" Laurel exclaimed. "I don't know what I'm saying, I mean, I don't know what I want to eat —" she broke off. Laurel closed the menu and handed it back to him.

"I'm sorry. I didn't mean to rush you. Would you like some time to decide? And while you're deciding may I bring you a glass of vino, perhaps?"

Laurel shook her head vigorously.

"No? Then a refreshing glass of lemonade

instead?" His smile was disarming.

"Yes, that would be lovely," Laurel murmured, still blushing, wondering why she was making such a fool of herself.

She comforted herself with the thought that she did not have to come here again — that is, unless she wanted to eat! Actually there was no other eating establishment close by where she could get such delicious, inexpensive food. Oh, dear! Then why had she chattered on like that? Was it because she seldom had a chance to talk to adults, only the children she taught? She tried to avoid her garrulous and inquisitive landlady except when the rent money was due, and she had not really made any acquaintances among the other roomers who all seemed much older and not especially friendly. This Gene was very nice. Besides, he was a student at the Conservatory, which gave them something in common. No, it wasn't as if he were a total stranger.

By the time Gene was back, Laurel had managed to recover some of her composure.

"I've consulted with Mario, the chef —" He wisked a tall frosty glass off the tray and set it in front of her with a flourish — "and he has suggested the perfect selection for a summer evening — a combination plate of prosciutto, chilled asparagus, fresh tomatoes, cucumbers, cheese, bread. May I bring it out for you?"

Dazzled by all this attention, Laurel could only nod again, hoping that the price of a "chef's choice" would not make it necessary to eat crackers and oranges in her room for the rest of the week. She watched him as he waited on other diners. He handled each one with the same affability as he had with her.

The attractively presented plate proved tasty and delightful as well as filling. As Laurel was finishing, Gene appeared with a chilled dish of pistachio ice cream, garnished with a thin chocolate wafer.

"Compliments of the chef!" He set it down on a small round lace paper doily.

Laurel started to protest. But Gene, glancing over his shoulder, laid his forefinger against his mouth. Laurel followed the direction of his glance and saw Mr. Pasquini standing at the cash register, nodding and smiling at them.

There was nothing for Laurel to do but eat the ice cream with relish. However, it left her with a dilemma. Did she leave a tip? From their brief conversation Gene must know she was on as slim a budget as he. Would he be insulted if she tipped him, after all his tactful kindness in serving her? Or would he naturally expect one? And what amount? While she struggled with this, Gene reappeared with her check on a small tray, then stood behind her chair as she rose, thanked him, and moved over to the cash register.

He waited at a discreet distance while she paid, then escorted her to the restaurant door, which he opened for her with a little bow. "It was a pleasure serving you, Miss Vestal. I hope we meet again."

It was not until Laurel was back on the sidewalk and had counted her change, that she realized neither the lemonade nor the pistachio ice cream was included on her bill.

Laurel was halfway down the block when she heard her name called.

"Miss Vestal! Miss Vestal, wait, please!"

She turned to see Gene Michela sprinting after her. Had she forgotten something? she wondered, stopping and turning around.

He reached her, flushed and panting. "Miss Vestal, beg pardon, if this seems too personal but — but do you attend church?"

Startled, she nodded, then quickly amended. "Yes, I do, but I haven't since coming to Boston. I mean, I don't belong to one —"

Gene shook his head vigorously and held up a protesting hand.

"What I meant was —" and he held out a

small card. "I'm singing at a wedding at this church next Saturday afternoon. It would be perfectly all right if you slipped in the side door and sat at the back." He smiled shyly. "I would like for you to be there . . . if you have no other plans."

Laurel looked down at the card he had handed her and read the scribbled name of the church, not knowing whether to laugh at this bizarre invitation. But Gene seemed so eager, so anxious, so appealing that her heart melted.

"Well, I'll try —" she began rather hesitantly.

"Oh, yes, *do* try." He smiled. "I'll sing as if you were there anyway!" Then with a wave of his hand, he backed away a few steps. "I've got to get back to the restaurant. I've diners waiting for dessert. Goodbye, Miss Vestal!" And he turned and ran back down the street.

What an astonishing young man, Laurel thought, amused. In spite of herself, in the days that followed, she found her thoughts turning more and more to Gene Michela. He certainly was impetuous and unconventional. Handsome, too, and terribly charming. Too good-looking, too assured, too charming?

Whatever conclusion she drew from this

impulsive act, on the following Saturday, a little before three, Laurel found herself entering the side door of an imposing stone building.

The church, one of the oldest in Boston, was tall and stately, set back from the street, surrounded by an iron fence. It was completely different from the small, white frame Community church in Meadowridge, and yet there was something strangely familiar about it, Laurel thought as she opened the door at the side entrance and slipped inside.

The interior was dim and quiet, for it was a good forty-five minutes before the scheduled ceremony. Down the long aisle to the front of the church, about ten pews on either side were bowed with white satin ribbon, obviously reserved for the wedding guests.

Laurel felt a bit like an intruder, but finding a seat in the rear, shielded by one of the stone pillars, she sat down. She occupied herself by gazing around at the arched stained-glass windows. Sunlight slanted through, giving the colors only a pale radiance. Each window depicted a symbolic event in Jesus' ministry — the Feeding of the Multitude, the Healing of Jairus's Little Daughter, the Good Shepherd and — Laurel drew in her breath as her glance moved to the next window — Jesus with the Little Children.

From out of her past a pale memory struggled to break through. She had seen that window before. Could *this* be the same church she had attended with her mother?

Laurel felt excitement tremble through her.

Here in Boston everything seemed like a giant link connecting her to her past, to her childhood. Maybe everything was leading her back to her roots, to her family, to her identity.

The deep tones of the organ reverberated through the empty church and with a start, Laurel realized that the organist had arrived and was testing his chords for the wedding music.

It seemed strange to Laurel to be attending the wedding of strangers. Yet a few minutes before the bride entered, when Laurel heard Gene's rich tenor voice filling the whole building with its glorious sound, she knew it had been worth overcoming her timidity to come.

Listening to Gene sing, the beautiful words of "O Perfect Love," Laurel felt little prickles along her scalp and down her spine. Truly *his* was a God-given gift and she thrilled to its splendor. There was more to that young man than she had thought. Much more! One could not sing with such a voice and not be aware of its Creator.

Tears welled up in Laurel's eyes. Coming into this church, seeing the window, hearing Gene's voice had been an emotional experience. Before the wedding ceremony was over, Laurel rose and left quietly. She was too deeply moved to chance meeting anyone, especially Gene Michela.

In spite of herself, Gene was much in her thoughts over the next few days. But she carefully avoided Pasquini's Restaurant for a few days, not wanting to appear to be encouraging special attention from Mr. Pasquini's part-time waiter!

Still most of her thoughts that spring were centered on Mrs. Maynard. Week after week Laurel was drawn back to the street where the Maynard mansion stood. She would sit on one of the benches in the shady park across from it, staring at its impressive facade. If this *was* her mother's family home and Mrs. Bennett Maynard *was* her grandmother, would she not have wondered all these years what had happened to her own daughter? Surely, if Laurel presented herself, wouldn't she be happy to see her granddaughter at last? Or did she still harbor the old resentments? Had she cut off her emotions concerning the daughter as completely as she had cut off communication with her?

April passed into May, May into June, and each time Laurel took the long trolley ride, there was no sign of any activity around the house. Apparently the occupants were away.

During her "visits" Laurel pondered how she would go about contacting Mrs. Maynard upon her return to Boston in the fall. She had no desire to shock her. No, first she would send flowers and a note, saying she had reason to believe they were related and asking if she might call.

Of course, there was no way of knowing what Mrs. Maynard's response would be. What if, after the flowers and note, there was no answer? If not, Laurel decided, she would follow up with another note and, armed with a copy of her parents' marriage certificate, and her birth certificate would simply go to the house and ask to see Mrs. Maynard. Of course, it was very possible the woman would refuse to see her.

Then what would Laurel do? She could only guess that the old woman's curiosity would be aroused. Certainly Laurel's resemblance to her mother would not go unnoticed or overlooked. Then she would show her the pictures in the heart-shaped locket. After that, surely there could be no mistaking who she was.

Still, Laurel knew she should prepare herself not to get that far. Could she be satisfied that at least she *had* found her parents' graves, proof that they were married, that she was their daughter and their rightful heir?

The rest of the story, the lost fragments of her early life and background she had pieced together. Her parents — the wealthy debutante and the struggling artist — had fallen in love and risked everything to be together. How they had met was still a mystery. But Laurel knew that until her father's death, her mother had been happy with her choice. Why, after Paul Vestal's death, the young widow had never been reconciled with her family, Laurel did not know. Surely there had been no reason why their daughter had lived on the edge of poverty when the Maynards were perfectly capable of providing for her. The cold hard truth might be they had never forgiven Lillian for what she did.

As Laurel sat contemplating the austere, shuttered house across the street, she asked herself if it were possible, after all these years, for the needless bridge of bitterness to be crossed? And what did *she* herself actually want from all this? She searched her heart honestly. She wanted nothing. Nothing, more than the Maynards' acknowledgment that she existed.

With summer coming, Laurel had more immediate worries. Her pupils' long vacation would deplete her small savings and soon it would be time to register at the Conservatory to audition for acceptance as a student for the coming year. Even with all her scrimping, Laurel had not been able to return Dr. Woodward's checks.

Knowing that the new schedules for classes, auditions, and list of coaches would be posted before the opening of school, Laurel went to the Conservatory one sultry day in June.

In the Administration Office she spent a great deal of time filling out forms. She hesitated a long time over the question: "Who will be responsible for your tuition, to be paid before the start of each semester?" Laurel did not want to write in Dr. Woodward's name and yet, if she wrote her own, the next questions "What is your employer's name. The source of your income?" would have to be answered honestly.

Would she have to wait another six months before applying to become a student, when she was assured of having enough money to pay for it? And what about finding and paying a coach?

Laurel sighed and shoved all the papers into the portfolio in which she carried her music, and decided to think everything over before completing her application. Explaining briefly to the woman behind the reception desk that she would be back later, Laurel started out of the office. As she did so, she bumped into someone just entering. Her portfolio fell from her grasp onto the floor, sending her music sheets flying every which way. As she stooped to retrieve them, so did the newcomer and, in their combined attempt to gather up the papers, their two heads banged together.

For a moment Laurel was stunned. Dizzily she looked up and saw the other person holding his forehead, a pained expression on his face. As they stared at each other, his look of discomfort changed to one of amused recognition and with mock indignation he demanded, "Miss Vestal! Don't you ever look where you're going?"

"Oh, my goodness! Mr. Michela!" she exclaimed.

In her confusion Laurel bent down again in an attempt to pick up the scattered music and so did Gene. They bumped heads a second time. This time they both collapsed into fits of helpless laughter. As their laughter rose, surrounding them in a sensation of idiotic delight, their eyes met and a remarkable thing happened.

Why, it's like something straight out of a romantic novel, Laurel mused.

Of all the people in Boston, of all the possible students at the Music Conservatory, of all the days of all the weeks of the summer, why had her path crossed so often and so unexpectedly with that of this charming young man?

As this question flashed through Laurel's mind, all her girlish dreams of falling in love came into focus. She had imagined how it would be to meet the right person, had hoped that person was Dan, had mourned when it was over between them, had nurtured a secret hope that someday, in some strange new place, she would meet someone else. Now he was here. And it was not a dream!

17

It seemed natural for them to leave the administration office together, walk through the lobby and out the front door of the building into the blinding sunlight.

"It's really good to see you again, Miss Vestal," Gene said, "or should I say *bump* into you again?"

"I'm not always so clumsy, believe it or not!" Laurel laughed as she paused at the stone balustrade and set down her portfolio so she could tighten the ties. Without raising her eyes from the task, she said shyly, "I heard you sing."

"*Did* you?" Gene sounded pleased. "I so hoped you would."

"You *are* very good, you know." Laurel continued checking the ribbons of her portfolio to see if it was closed securely. "You really have to sing, don't you?"

"It's my life!" he replied.

"It shows," she said seriously, at last looking up at him.

Gene's dark eyes sparkled with enthusiasm as he suggested they sit down on the steps in the sunshine. Suddenly they seemed to have so much to say to each other, about music, about themselves. Gene told Laurel he had just returned from a month's tour with a choral group.

"It gave me a taste of what a concert singer's life would be like. On the road two weeks at a time, trying to sleep sitting up on a day coach, staying at run-down hotels, terrible food!" He laughed. "For an Italian boy the latter has to be the worst of all! Speaking of food, I'm hungry. How about you?"

It was past noon, and Laurel realized she had had nothing since breakfast.

"Come on." Gene stood up and held out his hand to her. "Let's go get a hot dog."

At the concession stand a ruddy-faced man in a limp chef's cap and apron, took their order. He forked sizzling weiners into long buns, then slathered them with mustard.

"My treat!" Gene held up his hand warningly when Laurel opened her purse. "Not that the menu is very elegant, but just wait until I have my debut at La Scala! Then we'll really celebrate!"

Buoyed by his playful optimism — that he would actually one day perform at the famous Italian opera house and she would be with him on that occasion — Laurel held their hot dogs while Gene bought two bottles of soda. Then they found a bench and sat down to eat.

As they continued to chat, Gene mentioned names of composers and famous singers as if they were close friends. Laurel found all this fascinating even though, by comparison, her own knowledge was very limited.

After they finished eating, they walked along the flower-bordered path down to the lake. Gene took off his jacket and spread it on the grass for Laurel to sit on. They went on talking as though they had known each other forever, yet in their conversation was the excitement of discovery.

The afternoon was slipping away when suddenly Gene scrambled to his feet.

"Laurel, I'm sorry, but I didn't realize it was getting so late. I can't take you home, or I won't make it to work on time!" he exclaimed. "It's not such a great job, but I need the money."

"Then maybe I'll see you later at the restaurant."

"Oh, this is a second job — just temporary. I'm filling in for the regular who's sick." He seemed embarrassed. "I could make up something that would impress you, but the truth is I'm a night watchman at a warehouse."

"Oh, Gene, you don't have to try to impress *me!*"

"Of course you're right. My father always says all work is noble as long as it's honest."

"I believe that, too," she declared, although it was the first time she had thought much about the nobility of all work.

"But I did intend to take you home." Gene frowned. "I don't even know where you live. And I don't know how to get in touch with you — to see you again!"

"I can give you directions. You take the Number 10 trolley and —"

"Sorry, Laurel, but I don't have time to listen." Gene was already moving away, walking backwards as he spoke, "Could you meet me instead? Here? Tomorrow afternoon?"

"Yes!" she called. "Tomorrow afternoon! Right here." She nodded her head frantically as Gene, with a final wave of his hand, turned and made a run for it.

Laurel pressed both her hands to her mouth, giggling. How wild this was! And yet how happy she felt! She had not been this happy in weeks and weeks. She picked up her music portfolio and strolled in the other direction to the trolley stop.

She was still smiling to herself when she got off at her street and turned slowly toward the rooming house. Yes, this had been her happiest day since coming to Boston.

The next afternoon Gene was in the park waiting for her when Laurel arrived. Her heart gave a funny little flip-flop when she saw him pacing impatiently up and down. When he saw her coming, he broke into a big smile and rushed up to her, both hands extended.

"Laurel! I'm so glad to see you! I was afraid you might not come. To tell you the truth, I thought I'd dreamed the whole thing! The crazy way we kept bumping into each other — literally!" He threw back his head and laughed, a rich, full laugh. "And then last night, I kept kicking myself that I hadn't ditched the stupid job and seen you right to your doorstep. I thought maybe you'd think I was . . . I don't know . . . rude, irresponsible or something, and change your mind about meeting me."

Laurel shook her head. "Of course not! I told you I understood. Really!"

"Sure?"

"Positive." She laughed at his incredulity. "I wouldn't have come if I hadn't wanted to, if I thought you were . . . well, any of those things."

"Truthfully?"

"Yes, truthfully." She smiled. "Why don't you believe me?"

"I do." He squeezed her hands he was still holding. "Let's always promise to tell each other the truth, no matter what," he said earnestly.

Solemnly Laurel nodded, thinking how strange it was that it *didn't* seem strange at all for Gene to assume that there would be an "always" for them.

The rest of the afternoon flew by again. They never seemed to run out of things to talk about, to share and laugh about together. Gene had a wonderful sense of humor and was a raconteur. Everything that had ever happened to him seemed, in the telling, to be humorous, exciting, or an unexpected adventure. Laurel could not remember ever enjoying being with anyone so much.

By the end of the second day they had spent together, Laurel knew a great deal more about Gene. He had grown up in a small New England coastal town, part of a large, close Italian family with grandparents, many uncles and aunts and cousins. Although most of his relatives were fishermen, they were proud and supportive of Gene's pursuit of a singing career. Gene had won a scholarship to the Conservatory and had come to Boston right out of high school. But in spite of his paid tuition, he still had to work at odd jobs to support himself, pay for his coach, his rent. The Pasquinis, old family friends, were also kind, feeding him and giving him a job at the restaurant.

"Do you have a coach, Laurel?" he asked.

"No, not yet. I suppose I'll have to get one." She hesitated. "I — I really haven't done much about preparing for my audition either. Actually, hearing all you've done, all you've sacrificed to continue at the Conservatory makes me wonder about my own — well, my seriousness of purpose."

Gene looked puzzled. "I don't know if I understand what you mean —"

To her surprise, Laurel found herself confiding the roundabout way she had come to Boston. Her story just seemed to pour out, and before she knew it, she had told Gene the real reason for her move.

"I never really thought seriously about studying voice. But when my high school music teacher brought it up, it seemed like a good excuse to do what I'd been secretly planning all these years."

"And have you found out about your real family yet?" Gene asked.

Laurel told him what she knew.

"It's my grandmother, or the person I believe is probably my grandmother, that I still have yet to see." To be putting all this into words made Laurel realize she had never told anyone else in the world. And yet it seemed the most natural thing in the world for her to be telling Gene.

"I'm a little afraid, I think," she added.

"Would you like me to go with you when the time comes?"

Laurel felt the sweet surprise of his concern, the sincerity of his offer as if he were already a part of her life, and it touched her deeply.

As the days went by, they saw each other nearly every day, spending the afternoons together in the park. Within a short time Laurel realized being with Gene was the high point of her day — what she looked forward to each morning when she woke up, what she thought about the last thing before going to sleep at night. She was happier than she had ever been, happier than she had ever imagined possible.

Gene was everything Laurel wasn't —

outgoing, optimistic, enthusiastic. His personality complemented hers in every way. Gene's drive and ambition, his willingness to work hard to achieve his goals influenced Laurel to make a decision. Feeling she should cut her old ties of dependency to the Woodwards, she determined to get a job that would give her a *regular* income, not accept any more of Dr. Lee's checks. Only when she could afford it herself would she find a voice coach and apply to the Conservatory. It was the only fair thing to do, the only right choice.

Often when they talked together, sharing their thoughts, the deep things of their hearts, Gene would say, "Everything happens for a purpose, Laurel, nothing by chance! Like our meeting the way we did. There's a reason for it all. God has a plan for each of our lives. Nothing is an accident, although it may seem like one. I've always believed that. He gave me my voice so that I could not only make my living, but so I could contribute something to other people's lives, too. I'm never happier than when I'm singing. That's how I know I'm fulfilling His purpose for me."

Although not completely convinced herself, something that happened shortly after she made her decision to look for a job made

Laurel a believer. Taking what she thought was a shortcut back from the park to her rooming house one afternoon, she passed a Music Store with a sign in the window HELP WANTED, PIANIST.

On impulse, Laurel entered the store and found they needed someone to play the sheet music they sold to customers. When she sat down and sight read several pieces for the owner, Mr. Jacobsen, he hired her on the spot.

She could not wait to tell Gene the good news the next day. After congratulating her heartily, he told her he had some news of his own.

"Actually both good news and bad news."

"What do you mean?"

"Don't look so worried. The good news is I have a new job, a singing job! Just in the chorus, but at least I'll be singing. Gilbert and Sullivan. *The Pirates of Penzance.*"

"But that's wonderful, Gene!"

"Wait till you hear the rest." He held up his hand. "The bad news is that it's at a summer theater at the Cape."

"Cape Cod?"

"Yes, I'll be away for the rest of the summer — two weeks rehearsal, two weeks for the run of the show, maybe a chance to try out for the next one."

Laurel felt her heart sink.

"I hate the idea of being away from you," Gene said. "But, I can hardly turn down a chance like this."

"Of course, you can't," Laurel replied. "Anyway, it's only for a few weeks."

"That's right. The time will pass quickly."

"Yes, it will," Laurel agreed, not believing a word of it.

"I have to be there first thing Monday, so I'll leave Sunday on the morning train. But we've got today and Friday," Gene reminded her. "We'll go to the outdoor concert at Greenwood Gate Park on Saturday. We'll take a picnic supper and have a glorious last evening together. How does that sound?"

"Perfect." Laurel, already dreading the long separation, tried to sound happy.

Saturday afternoon Laurel dressed as carefully as if she were going to a ball. She chose one of the outfits Mrs. Danby had made for her the summer before and ironed it carefully. A short Spanish-style jacket of crisp, yellow cotton edged with trapunto embroidery, worn over a lawn blouse with delicate yellow featherstitching on the collar and cuffs, and a flared skirt belted with a wide green cumberbund. With it she would wear a basket-weave straw picture hat.

To avoid the probing curiosity of her land-lady, Mrs. Sombey, Laurel tried to slip down the stairs to wait for Gene outside. There he might also escape running the gamut of the ill-concealed envy and criticism of the other roomers who gathered in the parlor whenever there was the slightest chance of anyone having a "gentleman caller."

She was unsuccessful. As if on cue, Mrs. Sombey appeared in the lower hall just as Laurel was coming down. Her ferretlike face creased in a saccharine smile as she remarked with exaggerated sweetness, "Oh, my, Miss Vestal, how nice you look. I expect you're going out again with your young man? I *do* like to see my young ladies enjoy themselves," she purred. "And what a lovely ensemble! It looks very — shall we say, 'tray sheek'? Cost a pretty penny, I'd imagine," she simpered. "Or did you make it yourself, you clever little thing?"

When Laurel had first taken a room at Mrs. Sombey's, she had managed to say as little as possible about herself except that she planned to attend the Conservatory. But every month when she went to pay her rent, she was subjected to what she came to think of as an "inquisition." She was sure Mrs. Sombey investigated her mail, certain that she examined the postmark and return address on every letter.

Laurel had thought of moving, but this place was clean, quiet and convenient to the Conservatory, and since Mrs. Sombey only rented to women, Laurel had felt comfortably secure staying there. Except for the annoyance of Mrs. Sombey's insatiable curiosity, Laurel had been reasonably content.

It was just since Gene had come into her life that the landlady's interest in her comings and goings had begun to irritate Laurel.

Still it was not in her to be rude, so trying not to be as abrupt as she felt inclined, Laurel murmured a thank-you and proceeded to the front door. Before she reached it, quick as a cat, Mrs. Sombey was there, parting the curtains on the glass partition and peeking out.

"Well, here comes your fellow now, Miss Vestal. And he's . . . yes, well, I do declare, he's carrying a hamper. Does that mean you're going on a picnic? Well, my, my, how very —"

Laurel gritted her teeth, and not waiting for more, slipped out and hurried down the steps to meet Gene just as he came up to the house.

As usual, Laurel caught her breath at her first sight of him — the dark, windblown hair, eyes dancing with anticipation, smile lighting up his whole face.

When he saw Laurel, he stopped and put one hand on his breast.

"What a vision you are!" He said dramatically. "I should have brought you flowers!"

"Flowers?"

"Yes, of course! Flowers are the accepted gifts of courtship, aren't they? Instead, I brought you food!" Gene held up the basket. "Thanks to Mrs. Pasquini, who packed us a lunch you won't believe. I kept telling her there would only be two of us, but Benigna, who is a realist as well as a romantic, assured me that music stimulates the appetite."

"Come on." Laurel slipped her hand through his arm. "Let's be on our way before Mrs. Sombey thinks of some excuse to come out here and interrogate you!"

At the park, they roamed over the acres of rolling hills dotted with lovely old trees above the semicircular amphitheater where the orchestra would assemble later for the program. After a few minor debates as to the ideal spot, they agreed upon one. Gene opened the large wicker basket, took out a small rug and spread it out on the grass, tossing two pillows upon it. Next came a blue checkered tablecloth, plates, napkins and silverware. Then Gene began setting out a platter of thinly sliced ham, squares of cheese, small containers of black olives, cherry tomatoes, pasta salad, sliced cucumbers.

Laurel's eyes widened.

"My goodness, you were right. That's quite a lot of food!" she exclaimed, thinking of the limited diet she had been living on for the past weeks.

Gene was busy slicing a twisted loaf of crusty bread on a small wooden cutting board. "Well, you don't have to eat if you're not hungry," he teased.

"Oh, I'll force myself!" Laurel retorted, dipping a tiny tomato into a fluted bowl of dilled mayonnaise and popping it daintily into her mouth. She was getting better at the kind of bantering repartee Gene delighted in.

There was a container of chilled lemonade and another of strong Italian coffee to have with an array of fresh fruit as well as lemon tarts.

They ate with relish, talking and laughing, completely relaxed and happy in each other's company. Laurel tried not to think that the next day Gene would be going away for weeks. Every time the thought threatened to spoil things, she determinedly pushed it to the back of her mind. There would be time enough to miss him when he was gone. Now, it was enough to enjoy him.

"What will you have for dessert, madam?" Gene held up a bunch of glistening purple grapes in one hand, a perfectly rounded blushed peach in the palm of his other.

"Oh, I don't know — I'm so full but — why don't we share a peach?"

"No sooner said than done," Gene said, deftly cutting it through, removing the stone, and handing half the fruit to Laurel.

"Oh, it's so juicy!" she said, as she bit into the luscious slice. The juice ran down her chin and she tried to capture it with her tongue.

Whipping out his immaculate white handkerchief, Gene leaned forward and gently wiped her mouth and chin. He was so close Laurel could see the spiky thick eyelashes shadowing his brown eyes.

Then Gene said huskily, "Oh, Laurel, I can't remember what my life was like before I met you. Now I can't imagine it without you!"

She caught her breath. "I know. I feel the same way," she whispered, knowing it was true.

Then his firm, cool mouth was upon hers in a tender, lingering kiss.

As the kiss ended, Gene murmured, "I hear bells ringing, music playing —"

"I do, too," sighed Laurel. "It must be some kind of spell."

"It's called being in love," Gene said softly and kissed her again. Then he chuckled. "Truthfully, I think it's the orchestra tuning up their instruments. The concert will begin as soon as it's dark. We'll want to go down closer," he told her, getting to his feet.

Gathering up the remnants of their picnic, they repacked the hamper, picked up their pillows and blanket, and moved down the hillside.

The sky had turned a hyacinth blue and a faint evening star had appeared by the time they were settled. Soon the snowy-haired conductor marched on stage to the podium, rapped his baton and the first haunting strains of Vivaldi's *Four Seasons* rose into the evening air.

Gene was humming the melody from the finale as he and Laurel walked through the park and toward the trolley stop at the close of the concert. It had been a glorious evening and now Laurel felt melancholy, knowing it was coming to an end, that tomorrow Gene would be gone.

They were quiet on the ride back to the rooming house, holding hands, gazing into

each other's eyes with longing as the aware-
ness of the parting deepened. When they
got off, they walked the last block very
slowly, until they could delay the inevitable
no longer.

At the corner, Gene drew Laurel away
from the circle of light shining from the
lamppost into the shadows and took her
into his arms. His cheek rested against hers,
his lips moved along her temple, and she
heard him murmur her name.

She closed her eyes and felt him kiss her
eyelids, the top of her nose. Then he kissed
her mouth and it was sweet and thrilling beyond anything she had ever imagined.

"Oh, Laurel, I love you so," Gene whispered, then sighed, "but I have nothing to
offer you. I'm as poor as the proverbial
church mouse. Even with my scholarship,
and taking any odd job I can find, I barely
make enough to pay board and room, to say
nothing of my coach. It isn't fair when I have
no idea how or when —"

Laurel placed her fingers on his lips, shutting off the flow of words. Then she put her
arms around his neck, bringing his head
down against her cheek, wanting to comfort
and reassure him. Most of her life Laurel
had been sheltered, cherished, protected.
Now she was experiencing a new emotion

— a desire to give. A strange new tenderness filled her heart so full she could hardly speak.

"It doesn't matter. I'm poor, too, Gene. But we'll both make it. We'll help each other. I feel it, I *know* it. It will take time, but we're young, and we have all the time in the world!"

18

The week after Gene left for Cape Cod seemed endless. On her half-day off, Laurel took the trolley out to the secluded neighborhood where the Maynards lived. To her surprise she saw a gardener clipping the thick boxwood hedge and a man on a ladder washing the outside of the downstairs windows. Preparations were obviously underway for the return of the owners.

The sight of all this activity both excited and unnerved Laurel. After a sleepless night, she decided it was now or never. If she was ever to find out if Mrs. Maynard was her grandmother, she should not delay any longer.

Laurel had learned from Ava, whose garden was her hobby and delight, about the legendary language of flowers. Together, they had enjoyed making up arrangements to convey secret messages as was the custom in old-fashioned times. So when Laurel went to the florist shop to order the flowers she wanted to send Mrs. Maynard along with her note, she recalled some of those meanings. Whether or not the lady would understand their significance did not matter. It gave Laurel a feeling of reaching out in a special way.

After much deliberation she chose a mixture of gladioli and white peonies, softened with maidenhair fern, symbolizing strength, sincerity and discretion. Laurel placed the note she had labored over composing to be delivered with the box of flowers.

Dear Mrs. Maynard,

I am writing because I have reason to believe we are related. I am the daughter of Lillian Maynard and Paul Vestal, born in this city September 1884. If you would be so gracious as to receive me, I would like very much to call upon you so that we may discuss this possibility further.

Sincerely,
Laura Elaine Vestal

She used the double name on her birth certificate, which, she had been told, was given her in honor of her two grandmothers, though Laurel was not sure which of the two was Mrs. Maynard's name.

Underneath her signature, she had put the address of Mrs. Sombey's rooming house.

A week dragged by and every day Laurel hurried home from work hopefully. But no message came from Mrs. Maynard. She did, however, have one or two letters from Gene, all hastily written, telling of the thrills of rehearsals, the stimulation of being with other singers, and assuring her of his love. These she read over and over.

By the end of the week, Laurel resolved that she would not be put off nor would she wait any longer. There had been enough time for Mrs. Maynard to recover from any shock the note had given her and to consider the possibility that the writer *could* be her granddaughter. Now Laurel was determined to appear in person, and unless she was refused admission, she would confront her with the fact of her existence.

As she dressed for this momentous meeting, to bolster her courage, Laurel kept repeating to herself a Scripture verse she had memorized: "Ye shall know the truth, and the truth shall make you free."

It was as important for her as it was for

Mrs. Maynard to at last confront the past, acknowledge it, face the truth then — Well, however Mrs. Maynard chose to react, she, *Laurel*, would be free, no longer haunted by the possibility that her mother had never told her parents of her baby's birth. Maybe the estrangement had been too bitter, the parting too harsh, the pain too deep. Laurel remembered asking her mother once about the grandmothers for whom she was named and if she would ever meet them. Now she recalled the reply. "Someday . . . when all is forgiven."

Forgiven? Did Mama mean that she must forgive her parents, or that she needed *their* forgiveness?

At last, dressed in a dove-gray linen suit, a dainty white blouse, and wearing a polished straw hat ringed with white daisies, Laurel was ready. For a minute she stood thoughtfully, fingering the chain of her gold locket. Then she carefully pulled on white cotton gloves, picked up her handbag containing the copies of her parents' marriage certificate and her birth certificate, and went downstairs and out of the house. She walked resolutely to the corner of the street where she took the trolley out to the quiet neighborhood, to one household whose serenity she was about to shatter.

The butler answering the door was tall, his demeanor haughty. He held out a small silver tray for a calling card which Laurel could not supply.

"I have no card," she replied with what she hoped was suitable poise. Inwardly she was trembling. "But I think Mrs. Maynard will see me."

The man looked coldly suspicious. "Then whom shall I say is calling?"

"Miss Laurel Vestal."

"One moment, miss." He started to close the door, but Laurel slipped inside before he could leave her standing on the porch.

He gave her a withering look, turned sharply on his heel, and disappeared down the hall. Laurel clenched her hands together nervously. She strained her ears and thought she heard the murmur of voices coming from beyond the closed door at the end of the hallway.

Left alone, she looked around her. The foyer was oval in shape with recessed alcoves in which were placed marble busts. The parquet floor was partially covered by a runner of dark red carpeting extending from the doorway and up a broad staircase with wide polished banisters, leading to the second floor. At the curve of the balcony was a tall window with stained-glass panels through which a milky sun shed pale light into the otherwise shadowy interior.

It seemed an age since she had been left there, stiffly waiting, until the door at the end of the hall clicked, and she saw the figure of the butler returning. His expression had settled into what seemed to be permanent disdain.

"Although this is *not* Mrs. Maynard's regular 'At Home' day, she *will* see you," he addressed her in an icy tone. "Come this way, please."

Laurel followed, though the impulse to flee was strong. She fortified herself by remembering why she had come and why it was necessary to see it through.

At the end of the hall, the butler opened a door and announced, "Miss Vestal, madam," then stepped back for Laurel to pass into the room.

Her first impression was of overpowering ostentation — thick Oriental carpets, heavy carved furniture, gold-framed portraits on paneled walls. Then she saw that there were three people instead of the one she expected.

As she advanced a few steps, a man got to his feet and moved slowly behind the chair of one of the women. All of them were regarding her with curiosity and something else. Obviously she was an unwelcome intrusion, her ill-timed appearance interrupting a pleasant summer afternoon.

But at least *one* of them *should* have been warned of her coming. Laurel looked from one lady to the other. Which one was Mrs. Maynard? Which one was, possibly, her grandmother?

Her hands tightened on the tortoise-shell rim of her handbag. It somehow gave her strength, knowing that inside was the proof that she belonged here as much as any of them — or at least, that she had the right to come. "Ye shall know the truth and the truth shall make you free" flashed through her mind again, giving her added courage.

"Mrs. Maynard?" She spoke in a low, steady voice.

There was silence. The man made a slight impatient movement, as if shifting from one foot to the other. There was a moment's hesitation before one of the women spoke, "I am Mrs. Maynard."

Immediately Laurel focused her attention on the speaker.

Mrs. Maynard was thin, everything about her finely honed — the aristocratic nose, the unrelenting line of her mouth, the erect posture, the proud way she held her head, all bespeaking self-discipline and a certain inflexibility. She was a splendid-looking woman, who might have once been beautiful, Laurel thought, with her features, her beautifully coiffed iron-gray hair.

But as they regarded her, Laurel wondered what secrets were hidden behind those pale-blue eyes.

Then Mrs. Maynard spoke again. "This is my cousin, Mrs. Farraday, and her son, Ormand."

Only the man acknowledged the introduction with a nod. Mrs. Farraday merely stared at Laurel with wide-eyed annoyance.

"You wished to see me?" Mrs. Maynard's voice was cool with a distinct Boston accent.

"I am Laurel Vestal, Mrs. Maynard. You may recall I wrote to you a few weeks ago, asking if I might call?"

It was an effort for Laurel to keep her voice from shaking. She sensed she was on dangerous ground and that Mrs. Maynard was not going to make it easy for her. Nor did Laurel want to embarrass her in front of the two who were eyeing her visitor with undisguised suspicion.

When Mrs. Maynard did not reply, Laurel had to push further. "You *did* receive my note, did you not?"

Mrs. Maynard inclined her head slightly, but did not speak.

Laurel could sense the hostility mounting in the room and she rushed on hurriedly, before her courage failed altogether. "I have been waiting for an answer. When I did not hear from you, I decided to come in person."

There was a sharp intake of breath from the other woman, who straightened up in the tapestried armchair in which she was sitting. "The very idea!"

Laurel froze momentarily. No doubt she had committed some terrible social blunder. In this echelon of society, if someone did not reply to one's request to call perhaps it meant they did not wish to receive that person. But it was too late to worry about that now. She had come for some kind of answer, and she would stay until she got it. Unconsciously Laurel squared her slender shoulders.

Mrs. Maynard laid a restraining hand on her cousin's arm. "Gertrude, please, I'll handle this." Then waving one ringed hand toward a straight chair near the door, she asked, "Would you care to sit down, Miss Vestal?"

Still standing, Laurel suggested, "Perhaps I could come back at a more convenient time?"

At this suggestion, Laurel thought she

saw a flicker of relief in the otherwise rigidly composed expression. Mrs. Maynard rose from her chair. "Yes, perhaps that would be best. We are due at a meeting of the Symphony Society very shortly and as Chairwoman I cannot be late."

"Would you care to give me another day and time?" Laurel persisted, unwilling to let this opportunity pass without some definite commitment.

Mrs. Farraday made a clucking sound to indicate her irritation.

Ignoring her, Mrs. Maynard moved toward the door, extending one arm toward Laurel as though ushering her out. "I will send word when that can be arranged."

Having come this far, Laurel was not to be put off. As the older woman's hand rested on the doorknob, Laurel drew out the envelope containing the extra copies of her parents' marriage certificate and her birth certificate and handed it to her. "In the meantime, Mrs. Maynard, perhaps you would find these interesting."

The thin, controlled mouth seemed to quiver slightly, and there was a second's pause before she held out her hand to take the envelope.

When the drawing room closed behind her, Laurel heard Mrs. Farraday declare,

"The nerve of the girl!"

And in an entirely different context, Laurel agreed. It had taken nerve — all the nerve she could muster.

Outside again and in the warm summer afternoon, Laurel realized she had been holding her breath. She let out a long sigh. After the dimness of the shuttered interior of the Maynards' house, the bright sunshine was dizzying. She leaned against the brick wall for a moment to gain her equilibrium.

Well, it was done! She had carried out her part. The rest was up to Mrs. Maynard.

19

Laurel was thrilled to see a letter from Gene waiting for her on the hall table of the rooming house when she returned. She had never needed something to lift her spirits more. Gene's letters always did that. He wrote easily almost as if he were talking to her. From his descriptions of some of the people in the operetta cast, funny incidents that happened in rehearsals or even during the performances, Laurel could get a picture of backstage life.

She ran upstairs to her room, tore open the envelope, and devoured every word. But this letter was different from most of the others she had received from him. It was short and contained an unexpected message.

"I am making a quick trip to Boston. Since the theater is 'dark' Sunday and Monday, I'll leave right after the performance on Saturday night and be there some time Sunday. I have a surprise for you. I can't wait to show you."

Anticipating Gene's coming brightened what proved to be a depressing week for Laurel. Mrs. Maynard's promise to get in touch with her and arrange another meeting had not been kept. As each day passed without word, Laurel's disappointment turned into a kind of indifferent resentment. Their brief encounter had not endeared Mrs. Maynard to Laurel.

Maybe it was her own fault. Her expectations had been high. Laurel had imagined that once her grandmother saw her, recognized the unmistakable resemblance to her own daughter, there would be a joyous reunion. But it had been anything but joyous.

In spite of her initial cool reception by Mrs. Maynard, however, Laurel persisted in her desire to be acknowledged for who she was. Now it was much more than a validation of her identity; it had become a vindication of her parents' cause. Mrs. Maynard should take the responsibility for the unhappiness she had caused her daughter, for the way that courageous young woman had been forced to live — and die. She should face up to the fact that, because of her own arrogance and unforgiveness, her grand-daughter had been placed in an orphanage to be reared by strangers.

Though in her heart Laurel knew these were less than ideal motives, she held to them stubbornly.

The night before Gene's arrival, Laurel was restless. He had been away for so long — nearly three weeks now. What if he had found someone else among the pretty ac-tresses and singers in the cast? If not, there were always the summer people, many of whom entertained at lavish parties in their homes during the run of the play. Gene was so attractive, so talented. He was sure to be showered with flattering attention. The more she thought of it and of the mysterious note announcing his visit, the more Laurel imagined the worst. This, combined with the depressing circumstances of her heri-tage, sent her into an unaccustomed decline and she paced the floor, sleepless.

Toward morning, her gaze fell on the little slip of paper on which she had copied the Scripture verse she had memorized before her encounter with Mrs. Maynard: "Ye shall know the truth and the truth shall set you free." Well, she would soon know the truth about Gene, too, and about the love he had declared in his letters. Breathing a hopeful prayer, she fell into a deep sleep and awakened refreshed.

Rising hurriedly, she put on a pink linen that was one of Gene's favorites, then posted herself at her bedroom window to watch for him. While she waited she patted her hair distractedly, gave the bow on her sash an extra fluff, and fiddled with the frilled ruffle outlining her bodice.

He had mentioned a "surprise" in his letter. Just what kind of surprise? But she shook off the persistent dark thoughts. If she truly loved Gene, she would just have to trust him until he had a chance to speak for himself.

Spotting him coming down the street, Laurel flew down the stairs, slid the lock noiselessly back, and slipped out the front door. She was waiting for him at the top of the porch steps when he came through the gate, a square, brown paper-wrapped parcel under his arm.

One foot on the first step, he looked up at her, and her heart melted. He was regarding her with eyes filled with love, as if she were the only woman in the world. His mouth, parted in a smile, was as sensitive and sweet as she remembered.

"Hello, Laurel," he greeted her softly as she came down the steps toward him. "I've missed you, more than I can tell you, more than I thought possible."

Such a wave of relief swept over her that she was giddy.

"I've missed you, too, Gene," she confessed breathlessly.

"Then no one stole you away from me while I was away?"

The question was posed with such guilelessness that Laurel had to look deep into his eyes to be sure she had not asked it herself! Overcome by the irony of his question, Laurel began to laugh and soon Gene was joining her in a hearty duet, laughing uproariously.

"I see someone peeking through the curtains of an upstairs window," he said at last, when the last ripple of merriment had subsided. "Come on! Or I'll give Mrs. Sombey the first shock of the day by kissing you right here in broad daylight!" He grabbed her hand.

"Better not!" Laurel protested in mock alarm. "Or I'll be thrown out bag and baggage!" Then, in her best imitation of her landlady's voice, she said, "I run a respectable establishment, I'll have you know!"

And suddenly Laurel thought of Toddy. How like something her old friend would have said! Yet the laughter and the jesting had come spontaneously, bursting into bloom in the fertile soil of Gene's love, his approval. She felt so free!

"Let's walk over to the park where we can find some privacy and you can welcome me back properly," he suggested with a mischievous gleam in his eye.

After Gene's first suggestion had been carried out as promptly and satisfactorily as both had hoped, Gene put the package in Laurel's lap.

"Go ahead, open it," he directed, watching her eagerly.

"What is it, Gene? You shouldn't really be spending your money on presents for me." Laurel's fingers tugged at the knotted string.

"Stop fussing," he ordered. "Open it!"

She laughed and pulled at a knot. Impatient, Gene whipped out his pocket knife and cut the string. "There!" he said and Laurel tore away the paper.

For a minute she simply stared. Then she turned to Gene. She opened her mouth as if to say something, but no words came. Looking down at the contents of the package, she slowly put both hands on either side of the narrow wood frame and lifted the little painting from the box.

The canvas was small, perhaps twelve by

fourteen inches, the style Impressionistic. It might have even been a preliminary study for a larger, more detailed painting to be done later. This was done on the spot in daylight, without special attention to props or artificial lighting.

The subject was two figures — a woman and a sunbonneted child on the beach. The woman's face was shadowed by a wide-brimmed straw hat and the parasol she was holding; one graceful arm was extended to help the little girl make a mound in the sand. It was simple and heartfelt and absolutely delightful.

As Laurel gazed at it, a dozen emotions assailed her, prompted by the vaguest memories. In the lower right-hand corner were the tiny initials PV/86.

"Turn it over, Laurel," Gene said softly.

On the back, written with casual brush strokes, were the words — "August 1886, Lil and Baby L. at C.C."

Eyes brimming with tears, Laurel looked at Gene. "Where did you find this?" she asked in a barely audible voice.

Gene's face was animated as he replied, "In a little art gallery at Martha's Vineyard. I was just wandering around one afternoon when we didn't have a rehearsal. Actually, I was looking for some kind of little gift to bring you when I spotted this in the window."

"Oh, Gene, I'm sure this is one of my father's paintings!" Laurel exclaimed. "Do you suppose there are more?"

"I intend to go back and take a good look," Gene said seriously. "The new owner has stacks of unframed canvases in the storage shed behind the shop that he hasn't had time to sort through. He says this is one of the finest examples of Impressionist paintings he's seen."

"The style is very like the painting that hung over our piano when I was a little girl. The same sky and sand and feeling of lightness and a certain . . . serenity, I guess you'd call it." Laurel sighed, returning the painting to the box. "When I asked Mama why Papa painted so many seascapes, she told me that every summer a group of their artist friends would rent a house at the beach and take turns living there. It was something they looked forward to all year — a break from the humdrum routine of the rest of the year."

"Then we may be on to something. When I told this fellow, Ed Williams, that I knew the daughter of the artist, he told me he would get in touch with you when he had had a chance to evaluate all the paintings.

He seemed to think your father's work may be quite valuable."

"Gene, how can I ever thank you?" Laurel asked as she began rewrapping the canvas.

"Seeing you so happy is all the thanks I need." Gene took the package from her and retied the strings tightly. "In fact," he said, giving her a long look, "I want to spend the rest of my life making you happy."

Laurel held her breath, not daring to speak. It was a moment of knowing for them, a moment of decision, of choice and commitment.

"I love you, Laurel. I think I knew it from the first day. Do you . . . would you . . . can we be —" he faltered.

"Yes, yes, yes!" Laurel answered every question in a breathless rush. "I want that too. But how —"

"We'll work it out, my darling —" Gene drew Laurel close, kissing her with a new tenderness. When it ended, they searched each other's eyes as if in confirmation of the sweet promises they had just made.

Gene jumped to his feet, tossed his hat up in the air and caught it by its brim as it came sailing down again. "I'm the happiest guy in Boston!" He grinned.

"Oh, Gene!" Laurel sighed happily.

"I'm also the hungriest! Come on, let's go

get some breakfast!" He took her by the hand, tucking the wrapped picture under his arm and together they left the park.

Late that afternoon Laurel went to the train station to see him off again.

"No more of these partings," Gene told her. "I have enough money now to last me through the next semester at the Conservatory. I'm not going to take any more jobs that mean going out of town or on tour. That is unless —"

He halted, took both her hands and held them tightly.

"I want us to be married, Laurel, as soon as possible. I don't know how we'd manage or how —"

Caught up in his declaration, Laurel ventured, "I have my job and Mr. Jacobsen talked about giving me a raise."

Gene frowned. "But your own plans to start in at the Conservatory —"

She took a deep breath, casting about for words to express what was only now becoming clear to her. "Gene, I realize that I don't have the same urgent desire as you to pursue a career in music. That drive, that belief that my voice is my priority is just . . . missing. I love music, I enjoy playing and singing, but I don't think it could be the focus of my whole life. Not the way it must be to succeed. I just don't think I want it that much —" She paused, hoping he would understand. "Or maybe it's just that I've found I want something else more."

Just then the train whistle blew and the conductor was announcing, "All aboard!"

Pulling Laurel to him for a final kiss, Gene shouted above the noise of hissing steam and grind of gears. "I must go darling! See you in two weeks!" And he was gone, swinging up the steps and disappearing through the door of the car.

20

Two days later, Laurel propped the painting against the mirror of the bureau, then stood back to study it. She felt a deep thrill and pride knowing that Paul Vestal, the father she could not remember, was the artist.

She had recognized it as his right away. But she had not been prepared for her emotional response. Laurel ran her fingers lightly over the canvas, feeling the rough brush strokes. Looking at it, she could almost recall the warmth of the sand under the small bare feet of the chubby baby her father had captured in the painting. Strangely, she seemed to be experiencing again what could only be the vaguest kind of memory imprinted somewhere in the innermost part of her brain — the salty scent of the sea breeze bending the tall dune grass behind the figure of her mother, the clarity of the light, the cloudless blue of the wind-swept sky, the sun-washed roof of the weathered shingled cottage in the distance.

The fact that this painting now belonged to her, and that there might be more to come, sent a thrill shivering through Laurel.

The amazing coincidence of how Gene had found it made Laurel's head spin. She ticked off all the unrelated events that had brought this painting into her possession — What if she had not bumped into Gene on the steps of the Conservatory? What if she had never gone to Pasquini's to eat? What if they had not again collided in the administration office that day? What if? It could go on and on. Gene had not come into her life by chance, Laurel was sure of that now.

She thought of him now — back on the Cape — and the power of their love cast out all fear. He would be appearing in the next presentation of the summer light-opera series, with time to check again with the gallery owner to see if there were any more of Paul Vestal's paintings available. After the run of the second operetta, Gene planned to go to New Bedford for a short visit with his parents before returning to Boston. He was earning good money, and Laurel was proud he had been selected from the chorus of *The Pirates of Penzance* for the other show. She missed him, of course, but their time would come. Meanwhile, she was content to wait for him.

All this came back to Laurel as she stood looking at the painting. It all flowed together somehow — her coming to Boston to trace her heritage, her early plans for the Conservatory. Then she had met Gene and everything had changed. Her world circled around Gene now, everything else seemed less important. Finding a way to be together was all that mattered.

The next day when Laurel came in from work, Mrs. Sombey, twittering with excitement, was waiting for her in the downstairs hall.

"This came for you today, Miss Vestal," she said, her curiously light eyes protruding with greedy interest. "A handsome carriage drove up and stopped right out front and a driver in a fine, dark blue coat come right up to the door and asked if this was where Miss Laurel Vestal lived! When I said it was, he handed me this." Mrs. Sombey's hand was quivering as she handed Laurel a creamy vellum envelope with a red wax seal.

The handwriting on the envelope was in a fine Spencerian script, and Laurel knew instinctively it was from Mrs. Maynard. Not about to open it in front of Mrs. Sombey,

Laurel simply thanked her and started up the steps.

Mrs. Sombey's face crumpled with disappointment. Abandoning her usual put-on airs of prissy refinement, she blurted out, "Ain't you going to see who it's from?"

"Of course," Laurel replied over her shoulder, continuing to mount the stairway. She felt no obligation to satisfy her landlady's curiosity.

Ripping open the envelope, she noted the formal salutation:

My dear Miss Vestal,
    I have cleared my social calendar and will be at home Monday next from 3 to 5 in the afternoon if you would care to call. I shall send my carriage and driver if your reply is affirmative.
                    Cordially,
                    Elaine Maynard

Elaine! So *she* was the Elaine Laurel had been named for! She folded the note and replaced it in the envelope. Now that the long-awaited invitation had come, strangely enough it did not give her the satisfaction she had expected.

That evening she penned a reply as brief and impersonal as Mrs. Maynard's had been. She agreed to the meeting, but declined the offer of the carriage, stating simply that she would arrive on her own between three and four.

Coincidentally, the next day's mail brought a letter from Ava, the first Laurel had received from her since leaving Meadowridge.

My darling girl,

This letter should have been written months ago, but I was too preoccupied with my own sorrow. My main and inexcusably late reason for writing now is to assure you of my love and to ask your forgiveness if my actions caused you any needless guilt.

It has taken me a long time to face myself and to come to terms with the unhappiness I have caused those I hold most dear in the world.

For ten years you have given me enormous joy and never a moment's distress. You filled our home and my heart with more happiness than I ever thought I would know again. For this I am truly grateful.

Lee brought you home from the Orphan Train that day with the hope that you might take the place of our little daughter who died. Let me say you did not do that. Instead, you created your own special place and we could not love you more if you had been born to us.

Lee showed me the check you returned with your sweet note, saying you had been dependent on us long enough, and since you had left home without our approval, you did not feel it was right to continue accepting support.

How can I put this so you will understand? I was wrong not to let you go with a glad heart, allow you your freedom and your chance to be independent. It is your Papa Lee's and my pleasure to help you financially or any other way we can while you pursue your voice studies. We *are* your family and we want to support you wherever you are, whatever you choose to do.

I regret that my own sorrow at parting with you kept me from giving you my full blessing. I was like the Chinese princess in one of your favorite stories that I used to read to you, do you remember? She clipped the wings of her beloved songbird so he could not fly away and leave her. What happened, I'm sure you remember. The bird stopped singing! It is I who forgot!

So, now as you read this, I hope you realize that I, who love you so dearly, release you from the bonds I tied around you. Love should make us strong, capable and free to do whatever God's gifts enable us to do.

Be free, my darling, to be whatever you can be, desire to be, want to be. I believe, whatever makes you happy will bring happiness to others. I pray God's special blessing on you now and always.

Your loving mother,
Ava Woodward

Laurel read the letter over two or three times, savoring each sentence, almost memorizing each word. Her heart swelled with love and tenderness for the one who had written it. For this to have arrived the day before she was to meet with Elaine Maynard seemed remarkable. It gave Laurel the inner confidence she needed to face whatever the next day held for her. Regardless of her grandmother's attitude, whether she accepted Laurel or denied her did not seem quite as important, quite as necessary to her now.

Again Laurel dressed with exquisite care for her interview with Elaine Maynard. A navy blue silk with embroidered collars and cuffs, a matching straw sailor hat with crisp grosgrain ribbons, white gloves and dark blue handbag.

Her appearance and departure in the early afternoon caused more inquisitive glances and raised eyebrows on the part of Mrs. Sombey, who did everything but ask Laurel why she had not left for work that morning and where she was going now and if she could afford to lose a day's pay.

"When you wasn't down at the usual time, I almost come up to see if you was sick, Miss Vestal," the landlady said, her eyes traveling impertinently up and down Laurel, taking in every detail of her costume. "I know you always leave promptly at eight to catch the eight-fifteen trolley so you won't be late for work, so I couldn't help wonderin' —" Her voice trailed off, begging an answer.

Laurel smiled complacently and shook her head. "No, I'm quite well, thank you, Mrs. Sombey," she replied calmly and went out the door.

Her landlady would have been even more curious if she had seen that just around the corner, Laurel hailed a hackney cab and rode out to the Maynard residence in extravagant style.

It was precisely two minutes before three when Laurel mounted the steps and lifted the polished knocker of the front door. She turned and looked down the street at all the other fine houses lining this sedate enclave of the wealthy. There was a subdued splendor in the atmosphere, an understated but clearly defined exclusivity about the Square, setting it apart from the workaday world Laurel knew.

Standing there, waiting for the door to be opened, Laurel could not help wondering how different her own life would have been if Lillian Maynard had not been banished by falling in love with — "the wrong man."

"Good afternoon, miss," came a quiet voice from behind her, and Laurel recognized the same aloof butler of her last visit. This time he did not regard her coolly or skeptically, but stepped back immediately and opened the door wider.

At least she was expected, she thought, stepping inside.

"Mrs. Maynard will receive you in the parlor, if you will come this way."

The butler's manner was pointedly different, she observed, not condescending, but deferential. He opened the double door leading into a smaller room than the one into which she had been shown the last time. It was beautifully if less formally furnished, with a more intimate atmosphere, enhanced by the afternoon sunlight shining in. There was a piano in one corner, graceful chairs covered in needlepoint, bookcases flanking the fireplace, a hearth now hidden by a Japanese fan-screen.

"Good afternoon, Miss Vestal." Mrs. Maynard's thin, high voice greeted Laurel from where she sat in one of the high-backed chairs. She did not rise to offer her hand or in any way to make a gesture of welcome. She merely waved toward the opposite chair. "Do be seated."

Laurel tensed. All the confidence she had built up began to evaporate under Elaine Maynard's ice-blue gaze.

Mrs. Maynard seemed to be waiting for Laurel to speak first. Laurel, acting on some inner reserve, waited for Mrs. Maynard to open the meeting she had called.

Silence stretched between them. Mrs. Maynard's eyebrows lifted slightly. Then she spoke. "Well, Miss Vestal, I understand from your note you have some reason to believe we are related."

"Yes, Mrs. Maynard. I assume you have had time to look at the papers I left with you. They are copies of a marriage certificate and birth certificate — proof that my mother was Lillian Maynard and that *I* am your granddaughter." Laurel's voice was surprisingly steady.

Mrs. Maynard waved a dismissive hand.

"My dear young lady, certainly you must know papers can be forged! That is not proof of anything! What do you hope to gain by such a claim?"

Laurel was shocked. She thought she had prepared herself for any of several possible reactions from Mrs. Maynard, but not this cynical sarcasm.

"I have the originals —" she protested. She started to open her handbag, then remembered she had left them locked in her bureau drawer. She stared at Mrs. Maynard incredulously.

"Did you really think I would accept this? Someone walking in here off the street making all sorts of assertions? Do you take me for some kind of gullible, sentimental fool? Naturally, I would seek legal advice. I have my lawyer checking your shoddy copies. He was very skeptical of the whole matter, but promised to pursue it. But I *am* curious — what *did* you hope to gain by coming here and making this — this announcement?"

Laurel's slowly rising indignation at these insinuating accusations was suddenly overcome by a curious calm. She stood up.

"I did not come here for any reason other than to satisfy my own conviction that you are my grandmother, my mother, Lillian

251

Maynard's mother. I thought you would be glad, yes, *happy* to meet me! Perhaps, you never knew you even had a grandchild. Did you not ever wonder? Did you not care what had happened to your daughter after she left this house? After you drove her out?" Laurel's voice rose in spite of her effort to maintain her composure. "I look around me at this place, with all its luxury, all its obvious wealth — and I think of the shabby little flat where my darling mama and I lived, where she struggled to support us both by giving music lessons! And I wonder if you ever gave us a thought all those years! Did you know she died in the charity ward of a State Tuberculosis hospital? That I was put in an orphanage? And later on, an Orphan Train, to be adopted by strangers?"

At Laurel's words Mrs. Maynard visibly paled. Her mouth twitched and her bony hands gripped the chair arms until the knuckles were white and the huge sapphire ring flashed fiery lights.

"*Orphanage?*" she repeated.

"For two years I lived at Greystone Orphanage."

"*Greystone?*" The woman's jaw dropped slightly.

"Yes, Greystone . . . only a few miles from here, Mrs. Maynard." Laurel drew herself up, breathing hard, thinking of the cold stone buildings, the yards of bare floored corridors, the high curtainless windows.

"Mama never said a word against you or my grandfather, never explained why you had become estranged from her. I suppose she thought I was too young. Perhaps if she had lived, she might have told me the truth — that you could not find it in your cold hearts to accept the young man she loved. Could not accept the fact that their love was so strong she had to choose between him and her parents." Laurel's voice trembled and she shook her head. "I'm sorry for you, no, I *pity* you! You missed so much. You missed knowing a beautiful young man, a talented artist, who may still become famous! Worse still, you lost your only daughter —"

"Enough!" Mrs. Maynard put one shaky, blue-veined hand up, shielding her face. Her voice, sharp and keen as a knife, cut through the breathless words.

Laurel's whole body quivered with the strong emotions coursing through her. "Don't worry. I'm going now, Mrs. Maynard. If I upset you, I apologize, but I'm not sorry I came or that I told you the truth. Because it *is* the truth — all of it. You asked me what I hoped to gain by coming.

253

Actually nothing. I don't need anything you have, Mrs. Maynard. I have the tenderest memories of my real parents who loved each other and me dearly. I have loving adoptive parents, and I'm engaged to marry a wonderful young man. I don't need you. I don't want anything from you. Good day, Mrs. Maynard."

Still trembling, Laurel cast a pitying look at the old woman who was leaning to one side of the massive chair, her face covered with both ringed hands. Laurel moved toward the door. Her hand was on the knob when the imperious voice rang out once more.

"Wait! Stop!" A pause, then, "Please, Miss Vestal — Laurel, come back."

Struck by the change in the tone, the hint of a plea in the request, Laurel dropped her hand and, turning slowly around, faced Mrs. Maynard. The older woman's face looked deathly pale, almost gray, the eyes haunted.

"You are right. Lillian *was* my daughter. All these years I've tried to forget that — forget her, but — the minute you walked in that day, I knew it was impossible. You look so much like her — But it was a great shock. A terrible shock." Her hand shook as she put it up to her forehead where a vein in her temple pulsed. "I must admit my cousins, who were visiting that day, as you may recall, tried to convince me you were some sort of an impostor, a fortune hunter, urged me to have my lawyer check you out." She paused and toyed with the double strand of amethysts and pearls about her neck. "Of course, I followed their suggestion because . . . well because I hoped it was not true." She closed her eyes wearily. "You see, you must understand — it's been so long ago —"

Laurel did not reply, but listened.

"Lillian was our only child, born late in our marriage. My husband — my late husband Bennett — adored her. She was literally the 'apple of his eye.' A beautiful, happy child, a great joy to us — She was so gifted, so bright — Bennett took her everywhere with him. . . . We dressed her like a doll in French-made clothes . . . she was . . . exquisite —" Mrs. Maynard's voice broke.

After a moment she began to speak again.

"That's why it was so hard to accept . . . what happened. She was only eighteen . . . her whole life ahead of her — We were planning her debut, a magnificent ball, to introduce her to Boston society. It was all arranged when she told us she was in love —" Mrs. Maynard's voice grew strained, husky.

"Bennett flew into a rage, demanded to know how she had met this fellow. We had given her every advantage — piano lessons, voice and art lessons . . . it was there she met . . . Paul Vestal." The name was uttered with contempt. "When Bennett discovered he was her art teacher, penniless, with no background, no prospects, he decided he could not let her throw her life away. He forbade Lillian to see him — immediately made plans to take her away to Europe, hoping the distance between them would make her forget him, cool the romance. Of course, in retrospect, it was the worst thing he could have done. Lillian was sweet-natured but also strong-willed. And the result was on the eve of our sailing date, she ran away — eloped."

The room was still, absolutely quiet. Laurel waited for Mrs. Maynard to continue.

"Bennett never got over it. It broke his heart, hastened his death, of that I'm positive. And he never forgave her. He died only a year and a half later. He had forbidden me to answer the letter she wrote us after she was married, forbade me to contact her in any way." Mrs. Maynard sighed heavily. "I obeyed. What else could I do? I had always obeyed him. We had been married nearly thirty years, and that is how I was brought up to believe, that a wife obeys her husband."

Laurel said nothing and eventually Mrs. Maynard went on.

"Bennett suffered through a long agonizing illness. He lingered for months and I was with him almost every minute. When the doctors told me the end was near, I thought about Lillian, wanted to get in touch with her, bring her home to say goodbye to her father. But Bennett was adamant. When I suggested trying to find her, he got very upset, said we had no daughter. And he made me promise I would not ever attempt to contact her — even after his death."

Hearing this sequence of events, all the missing pieces she had wondered about for so long, Laurel was overcome. As she saw tears fill Mrs. Maynard's eyes and roll down the wrinkled cheeks, her heart wrenched. All this unnecessary suffering and sorrow. What a terrible, twisted thing so-called love could become.

"When last week my lawyer came to me, authenticating all the same things you said . . . that my daughter had died in a tuberculosis sanatorium, that there was a child —" Mrs. Maynard bit her trembling lip, dabbed her eyes with a dainty, lace-trimmed handkerchief. "But it was just now when you — you mentioned Greystone Orphanage that something inside me — to think I've been on the Fund-raising Board of Greystone Orphanage for years — and not to know my own grandchild was there, only a few miles away all the time —"

At this, Mrs. Maynard bowed her head and put both hands up to her face. Under the lacy shawl the old woman's shoulders shook convulsively.

All at once, Laurel was moved by compassion and in another minute she was on her knees on the floor in front of Elaine Maynard, her arms around her.

21

It was still light when early that evening, to Mrs. Sombey's complete astonishment, an elegant landau, glistening black with red-rimmed wheels drawn by a handsome dapple gray horse halted in front of her rooming house. The rig was driven by a haughty-nosed driver in gray broadcloth coat, black high hat, gloves and high shiny black boots. From her post behind her stiff, lace curtains she watched in open-mouthed amazement as he climbed nimbly down, opened the carriage door, and assisted one of her boarders out. When she saw it was Laurel to whom he bowed slightly and tipped his hat, she could hardly contain herself. So mesmerized was she by this unusual occurrence that Laurel was up the porch steps and coming in the front door before Mrs. Sombey had a chance to do more than back up a few steps to save herself a bump on the nose as Laurel opened it.

"Oh, Mrs. Sombey, I'm glad you're here," Laurel exclaimed.

Something was up, that was for sure, the landlady told herself, seeing the girl's flushed cheeks. Hastily she assumed nonchalance, flopping her feather duster, pretending she had been dusting the hall table all along. But Mrs. Sombey would never have guessed the explanation Laurel was about to give her.

"I'm moving out. I have just come to get my things."

"Moving out?" Mrs. Sombey repeated, nonplussed. "Just like that? Without giving any notice?" She drew herself up huffily. "I'm sure I had no idea you wasn't satisfied with your lodgings, miss. You certainly never gave the slightest indication —"

"Oh, it's not that, Mrs. Sombey. My room has been . . . well, fine . . . that is, until now. You see I'm going to stay with my grandmother on Wembley Square."

Laurel had no way of knowing what the name of that prestigious residential section meant to someone like Mrs. Sombey.

"Wembley Square?" she repeated through stiff lips. "Your *grandmother!* Well, indeed, Miss Vestal, you never said nothing about having relatives in Boston before. I thought you was — I mean, you being from the Midwest and all, I naturally assumed —" the landlady was, for perhaps the first time in her adult life, at a loss for words.

"I know. But it's really too complicated to explain, Mrs. Sombey." Laurel smiled apologetically and then breezed by her and ran up the steps. "I'll just pack up my things now. My grandmother's driver is waiting for me," she called back over her shoulder.

Indignant at being taken so off guard by all these unexpected events, Muriel Sombey vented her furious frustration by hurrying to the foot of the stairway and, losing her pseudogentility, shrilled up after Laurel's departing figure. "There'll be no refund for the rest of the month, Miss Vestal, you understand? If I'da known you was leaving, I could have rented that room twice over for what you've been payin'."

At the landing Laurel stopped and leaned over the banister, saying sweetly, "Of course, Mrs. Sombey. I understand. I did not expect any refund."

Laurel was not sure what awakened her — muted sounds from somewhere deep in the house, the snip-snap of a gardener's clippers in the garden just below the bedroom window. Or maybe it was the quietness itself, accustomed as she was to waking to the sound of delivery-cart wheels on the cobblestone street outside Mrs. Sombey's boardinghouse, the shouts of the drivers on the delivery wagons, the voices of the other roomers standing in line outside the hall bathroom, the repeated slam of the front door as they left the house on the way to work.

Laurel had noticed many times before the sedate pace of life on Wembley Square. Even the horseless carriages seemed to run noiselessly, while pedestrians moved with a purposeful dignity. The whole neighborhood exuded an aura of quiet charm and permanence.

In contrast, Laurel lay in bed in a kind of daze, thinking how quickly everything had changed since the previous afternoon. Three hours after her arrival at the Maynard residence, she had been on her way to her rooming house to pack up all her belongings and move in here with her grandmother!

"Grandmother," Laurel whispered the word, feeling its taste on her lips as she said it. Mama's mother.

Her eyes roamed the room, sweeping up through the lacy crocheted canopy of the dark mahogany four-poster to the little desk between the two windows, the small white marble fireplace. Mama's girlhood room, where *she* had slept — in this very bed — played with her dolls, studied her lessons, dreamed her romantic dreams! Here, in this spot!

After all the years of imagining, the reality was almost overwhelming. Laurel sighed and stretched, then snuggled once more into the lavender-fragrant sheets, the satin-covered feather quilt.

When she had returned with her belongings last evening, Laurel had found Mrs. Maynard looked very tired. They had a quiet supper together before the fire in the small parlor — delicious, delicate food, well-prepared and tastefully served. But neither of them had eaten very much. At length Mrs. Maynard had regretfully admitted, "If you will excuse me, my dear, I really think I must retire. This has been quite an emotionally exhausting day for me. I'm no longer young nor very resilient, I suppose."

"Of course, Grandmother, I understand."

Mrs. Maynard rose and passed by the place where Laurel was sitting. Laying her hand, as light and dry as a winter leaf, against Laurel's cheek she said, "At least I

263

can look forward to many such evenings with you in days ahead, and tonight sleep peacefully, knowing my grandchild is under the same roof." She sighed and seemed about to say something else, but did not. Then she drew from her pocket an envelope, yellowed with age, worn around the edges.

"I think you should read this, Laurel," she said. "I've kept it all these years, wept over it, if the truth be known, and wished with all my heart that I had acted upon my real feelings at the time. Maybe reading it will help you understand — Well, I'll leave that to you, my dear."

Her grandmother left the room in a lingering scent of violets. Laurel held the envelope, looking at the familiar handwriting. Even before she opened it, she knew who had written it. Carefully she took it out and, by the light from the fireplace, read the letter.

She had taken it upstairs to the bedroom and read it again before going to sleep. It was lying on the table beside the bed where she had put it, and now Laurel reached for it again.

With the early autumn sunlight streaming through the windows, Laurel read the words her mother had penned so many years ago, feeling her own young, in-love heart respond with special understanding.

Dearest Mother and Father,

By the time you read this, Paul and I will be a long way from Boston. We were married by a justice of the peace at the Court House a few days ago. It was not the church wedding I'd always dreamed of having, with my beloved and loving parents in attendance. But since you have made it clear that you would never accept Paul as the man I love and have chosen to be my husband, we felt we had no other alternative.

As you must know, I would rather have had your approval and blessing, but since you withheld it and declared it would never be forthcoming, I had to make the hardest decision of my life. It breaks my heart to have to choose between my parents and Paul, and I still feel it did *not* have to be thus.

I thank you from the bottom of my heart for my happy childhood and home and all the loving care, the many advantages and privileges you showered upon me. Whatever you may think now, I am not ungrateful.

I love you both dearly and never

wanted to hurt you in any way. I hope there will come a time when you will forgive me and know that you have not really lost a daughter but now also have a wonderful, gentle, kind, talented young man, willing and anxious to be a son to you both. Always,

Your loving Lillian

Laurel was still holding the fragile, thin sheets of paper when a soft tap came on the bedroom door, and a maid in a ruffled cap and apron peered in.

"Morning, miss. Just came in to light the fire and warm up the room before you got up, then to tell you your grandmother would like you to join her for breakfast."

Laurel sat up smiling and motioned the young woman regarding her so curiously to come in. She guessed the household staff was all agog over the news of the sudden, unexpected appearance of a Maynard granddaughter.

One of the first notes Laurel wrote, seated at her Mama's little desk in her former bedroom, was to Gene.

"You are simply not going to believe all that has happened to me since you left," she wrote. "You will first wonder at my change of address, I know, so I must tell you the wonderful thing that has happened."

Laurel's pen skimmed over the stationery as she told Gene all that had taken place since they parted. "I can't wait until you meet her! She's very grand, so be prepared! Most of all, I want *her* to meet *you.*"

If Laurel's letters about her new life with Mrs. Maynard were exuberantly enthusiastic, they only reflected her own euphoria. One day followed the other in a kind of sunlit splendor. Mrs. Maynard had so much to show Laurel — keepsakes, photos, the portrait that had been painted of Lillian as a child and had once hung over the fireplace in Mr. Maynard's study, even her baby clothes that had been kept in a locked trunk. They spent many happy hours together, poring over these and albums and scrapbooks of Lillian's school days.

"You can see why it was such a blow to us, can't you, my dear?" Mrs. Maynard would ask Laurel over and over. "To lose her was like losing a part of ourselves."

Laurel longed to ask why it was necessary, why they had never given her father a chance, never even met him. But the harmony existing between her grandmother and herself was so comforting, so sweet, Laurel was loath to break it. There would be time for some of those hard questions later, after they were better acquainted. Just now they were moving slowly, cautiously into this new relationship.

Afternoons were spent in any number of pleasant ways — a carriage drive in the afternoon, or shopping in some of the lovely, exclusive stores where Mrs. Maynard was immediately recognized or stopping for tea at one of the luxurious hotels where they were always greeted by the maitre d' and ushered to Mrs. Maynard's special table overlooking the park, now brilliant with autumn colors. Here they were served by solemn, uniformed waiters an elaborate medley of dainty sandwiches, hothouse strawberries dipped in chocolate, truffles or glazed fruit flan or iced petit fours, with fragrant oolong tea.

Sometimes in the evenings, at Mrs. Maynard's request, Laurel would play the piano for her.

"You have Lillian's musical talent, that's evident," Mrs. Maynard sighed. "You must go ahead with your plans to attend the Conservatory. Of course, I will take care of all your fees, arrange for a coach —"

Laurel began to feel like Cinderella. What would Gene think of all these offers? Would her grandmother's generosity extend to him? He was actually the one with the *real* talent. She had mentioned him often, but her grandmother had not seemed interested in pursuing the discussion. In fact, she seemed to have forgotten all about Laurel's engagement. There was so much else to talk about and enjoy together. Her grandmother liked to play chess and taught Laurel the intricacies of the game. With their time so pleasantly occupied Laurel did not notice how quickly it was passing until one day she received a short note from Gene, saying he would be back at the end of the week.

"And where did you meet this young man?" Mrs. Maynard asked, a slight frown puckering her thin, high-arched brows.

"At the Conservatory, Grandmother," Laurel replied, deliberately omitting an account of the unorthodox manner in which she and Gene had really met. Somehow Laurel did not think Elaine Maynard would approve of so casual an introduction. Neither did she tell about their further meeting at Pasquini's Restaurant where Gene waited on tables.

On this afternoon when Gene was expected, Laurel and her grandmother were in the small parlor, awaiting his imminent arrival. Mrs. Maynard was seated in her favorite wing-back chair, her hands busy with needlepoint while her eyes keenly observed her granddaughter. Laurel was too excited to sit down. Everything about her fluttered — the ruffles on her skirt, the tendrils of waves escaping from her coiled hair, the handkerchief she carried as she moved back and forth from door to window.

"Do light somewhere, child. You are as nervous as a butterfly," complained Mrs. Maynard.

"I'm sorry, Grandmother. It's just that I'm so anxious for Gene to come, for the two of you to meet." Laurel turned a radiant face on her. "Oh, I know you'll be impressed. He's so handsome, so charming, has such a wonderful personality. And, oh, Grandmother, you should hear him sing!" Laurel sighed rhapsodically.

"Is he planning a professional career?" was Elaine's next question.

"Oh, that's inevitable! He has a glorious tenor voice. He's already been on tour twice — only in the chorus, up till now. But a career has to be built slowly. This summer at the Cape theater he was in *The Pirates of Penzance*."

Mrs. Maynard pursed her lips. "Very few ever actually make it, you realize, don't you, Laurel? Only the very best, and that after years of training and study, and certainly a year or two in Europe —"

"Oh, I have no doubt Gene will make it. He is determined and certainly has the talent."

"But does he have the means to finance such a long period of training, a family willing to support him until he is at a point where he can demand . . . shall we say . . . a living from his voice?"

Laurel hesitated. Should she tell Mrs. Maynard that she knew very little about Gene's family, only that they were hard-working Italian fishermen, that Gene had to work at menial jobs to support himself, that they had already discussed the future of his career and her part in helping him attain his goals?

Even as she considered how much to confide of their plans, the sound of the knocker echoed through the downstairs. A bold, confident knock. Laurel smiled, thinking that neither fancy facades, shiny brass knockers, nor formidable butlers would ever intimidate Gene. She started over to the parlor door, ready to rush into the hall.

"Thomas will show your guest in, Laurel," her grandmother said sharply.

Laurel halted, surprised by the reprimand in Mrs. Maynard's voice.

A minute later there he was, right behind

271

the solemn Thomas. Laurel's heart spun at the sight of him. He looked marvelous, his skin still attractively bronzed from days on the beach. Nor could her grandmother fault his attire. He was dressed for the occasion in a light beige twill suit, crisp striped shirt with snowy stiff collar, a waffle-straw hat tucked under one arm.

Laurel swelled with pride as she reached for his hand and drew him into the parlor. Then, turning to Mrs. Maynard she introduced him.

"Grandmother, I'd like you to meet Gene Michela. Gene, my grandmother, Mrs. Maynard."

Elaine held out her hand and Gene walked over and bowed over it as he spoke in his clear, rich voice. "A pleasure, Mrs. Maynard."

"Mr. Michela." Elaine was politely formal. "Please be seated. Laurel tells me you have spent the last several weeks at the Cape."

It was only then that Laurel was conscious of the chill in the room. It was as if someone had opened a door and a winter wind had swept through. Somehow Mrs. Maynard had deftly taken control of the conversation and begun to conduct what amounted to an interrogation. The situation took Laurel unawares at first, but once she had grasped what was happening, she grew tense with anxiety.

Thomas brought the tea service in on a round silver tray and set it down on a low table in front of Mrs. Maynard. Alerted that Gene was under some kind of scrutiny, Laurel watched with mounting apprehension as he took one of the dainty napkins, flicked it open, placed it on his knee, asked for lemon instead of cream, accepted one of the tiny triangles of watercress sandwiches, answered all Mrs. Maynard's probing questions with ease and never with his mouth full. Laurel was ashamed of herself for fretting. Under any other circumstances, it would never have occurred to Laurel to worry about the kind of impression Gene was making. He was always the perfect gentleman, had impeccable manners. Still, it was her grandmother's unrelenting observation that made Laurel uneasy, and she couldn't help the image that came to mind — that of the spider spinning her fatal web.

Then quite unexpectedly Laurel heard her grandmother say as though puzzled,

"Michela? Is that an Italian name or perhaps Portuguese? I understand there is quite a large Portuguese population in the coastal communities. Where did you say you were from originally? New Bedford?"

Laurel snapped to attention. She felt a strange sense of déjà vu. Of time turning backward. Weren't those the same words her grandmother had quoted Bennett Maynard as having said in the confrontation with her mother so long ago? A confrontation that had probably taken place in this very room!

"Paul *Vestal?* What kind of name is *Vestal?* Polish? Hungarian? Is he from one of those Balkan countries always in revolution? How long has he been in this country? A year or two? You mean he's an *immigrant?* Lillian, your ancestors came here on the Mayflower! Men of quality, old families, men of the cloth, lawyers, teachers — you have a long and illustrious lineage. And you want to marry this man with no background, some *foreigner?*"

She imagined the same icy tone she was hearing now in Mrs. Maynard's voice, and felt a blaze of anger ignite within her. How insulting Mrs. Maynard was being in her cool, civilized "drawing room" manner! Laurel glanced over at Gene to see if he was feeling it, reacting to it. But he looked perfectly relaxed, listening to Mrs. Maynard with polite attentiveness. Of course, he was too sensitive not to feel the sting, but too

274

gracious to show any emotion. He was be-having as a perfect guest. It was her grand-mother who was taking advantage of her position as hostess. Hostess? The Grand In-quisitor, rather! Gene was not on trial here, Laurel thought indignantly.

Or was he? Quickly Laurel remembered an enigmatic conversation she and her grandmother had had over tea one after-noon. Mrs. Maynard had remarked casually that soon she wanted to introduce Laurel to some young people of her acquaintance, daughters and sons of some friends in "our set."

So that was the game? She was trying to prove Gene unsuitable. No wonder she had ignored Laurel's mention of her engage-ment.

Laurel felt a chilling reality, as if a smoth-ering cloak, were dropping over her head, almost heard the clang of a trap bolting, locking her in, shutting Gene out. It was his-tory repeating itself. Lillian and the unsuit-able "foreigner" Paul Vestal all over again. But this time it was Laurel and Gene Mrs. Maynard was trying to break up.

Laurel felt her smile freeze on her lips as she sat there holding the delicate handle of her teacup balanced on her lap. Her eyes moved from Gene to her grandmother, back

275

and forth, like watching a tennis volley. She was pleased to see that Gene was holding his own, replying to all Mrs. Maynard's outrageous questions with complete poise.

Her heart warmed and melted. What a true gentleman he was! Never mind he was probably not measuring up to all her grandmother's invisible criteria, possibly missing the mark of her prerequisite targets for approval and acceptance. What did that matter? Her mother had been brave enough to withstand such pressure, to follow her own heart, to find happiness with the good man she had loved and married. Laurel remembered Mama saying once that to have known even a short time of perfect happiness was worth the sorrow she had known afterwards.

Apparently her grandmother was only looking for shallow externals. In Gene, Laurel had found more than a pedigree or even a handsome face and courtly manners. In him, she had found inner goodness, gallantry, lasting values.

Then Gene was on his feet. "I must be on my way now, Mrs. Maynard. Thank you for allowing me to visit Laurel here, and for the honor of meeting her grandmother."

Laurel rose with him. Setting down her cup, she said, "I'll walk you to the door. Excuse us, Grandmother." She slipped her hand through Gene's arm and together they went out of the parlor and into the hall.

"Gene," she whispered, "I want you to meet me tomorrow at our old place in the park. We must talk, make plans. It is impossible here."

He squeezed her hand, his eyes darkening with understanding. "Yes, of course. I'm working tonight at the restaurant and a private party tomorrow night, but shall we say two tomorrow afternoon?"

"I'll be there."

Laurel did not return to the parlor but went upstairs to her bedroom. She closed the door, went over to the window, and watched Gene's departing figure on his way to catch the trolley.

"I love you!" She blew a kiss, then turned and resolutely got out her suitcase and began packing.

22

Gene was waiting for Laurel when she arrived in the park, flushed and breathless from hurrying. He caught both her hands and raised them to his lips. Then, putting his arm around her waist he led her over to a bench where they sat down.

"What is it, darling? What's troubling you?" he asked, all tender concern.

In as few words as possible, Laurel explained her feelings. "It's almost eerie, Gene. It's starting all over again, just like it was with Mama — at least, the way I imagine it was with Mama. My grandmother doesn't even realize what she's doing." She paused, looking worried. "I don't want to hurt her, but of course I can't stay." She hesitated, not wanting to tell Gene it was specifically Mrs. Maynard's attitude toward him that had brought about her decision. "I don't want to go back to Mrs. Sombey's, so I must find another place to live."

Gene was silent for a minute, his brows furrowed as if in deep thought. Then he said slowly, "This is too important a decision to make impulsively, Laurel. You've waited too long to find your mother's family to walk out."

"But —"

"Wait, let me finish." Gene held up his hand to stem her protest. "Granted, your grandmother is old and set in her ways. She's used to managing things, servants, other people's lives. Your leaving won't change her, Laurel, except in ways you don't want to be responsible for. I could see you mean a great deal to her. After so many years of denial, having you, her own grand-daughter in her home . . . can't you see? It's given her a new lease on life. Of course, she's full of plans for you. Just think what her life must have been like all these years before you came. Think —" he lifted her chin with his thumb and forefinger and searched her face — "Think what they will be like if you leave her now."

"But, Gene, she wants me to become something I'm not! At least Mama was raised to be a socialite. I wasn't." She smiled ruefully. "And I used to think Mother — my *adoptive* mother — was possessive!"

Gene laughed. "See?"

"But what shall I do?"

"I think you should be patient with her — gentle and understanding the way you always are. Give your grandmother time to get to know you. Gradually she will loosen the tight grip she has on this newfound happiness. Right now, she's afraid it will slip out of her hands, and that would be like losing her daughter all over again." When Laurel began to weep quietly, he held her close. "Don't worry, I'll help you darling. Together we can win your grandmother over. I'm sure she doesn't want to make the same terrible mistake *twice*."

"Yes, I suppose you're right, Gene — in fact, I *know* you are." She sniffled and he whipped out a huge white handkerchief to mop her tears.

He took Laurel's hand, smoothing out the fingers, one by one.

"It may be a few weeks before everything can be worked out . . . and I didn't want to say anything about it until I was sure. But there's a very good chance that I'm going to be hired by the Conservatory as one of their coaches on a good salary plus, of course, coaching fees. If that happens, we could get married right away." He looked at her hopefully. "Unless you've changed your mind?"

"Of course I haven't changed my mind. But can we really afford it? To get married, I mean? We discussed it before and never thought we could. This wouldn't mean your giving up your singing career, would it? I wouldn't want to do anything to delay your dreams coming true."

"Laurel, don't you know by now? You *are* my dream come true! You *inspire* me, make me want even more to succeed, in my career. Actually, this would provide me with more time on my own to practice, study languages, like German and French for example, in which so many operas are written. But the main thing is, we would be together." He raised her hand and kissed it. "Besides that, I have some very good news for you from Ed Williams, the owner of the art gallery at the Cape."

Laurel was all eager attention.

"I didn't know this before, but he has a gallery here in Boston. He has a partner who is actually an expert, a real art expert and critic. It seems his partner came up to look over this cache of paintings I told you about, your father's among them." Gene paused significantly. "Well, this other gentleman, Karl Sandour is his name, became very excited when he saw Paul Vestal's paintings. There are quite a few — most of them beach scenes — very light, vivid colors, local scenes, families and children, all in very natural, appealing settings. Williams's partner, this Mr. Sandour, wants to have what they call a retrospective of American Impressionists and particularly of your father's Cape Cod pictures."

"Oh, how wonderful, Gene! But —" her sunny smile faded — "I wish it could have happened while he was living."

"Yes, well I'm sure he would be happy to know the daughter he painted so often will be receiving the benefits."

"What do you mean?"

"Williams and Sandour want you to see all the paintings, decide which ones you want for yourself, then give them permission to put the others on exhibition and for sale. They will take care of all the expense of cleaning the canvases, framing them, the cost of brochures, advertising, everything, and of course they will take a percentage of all sales." Gene paused again and said quite carefully. "But from what they tell me, Laurel, even with that, you should be a very wealthy young lady."

Laurel stared back at Gene. It was taking a long time for all he had said to sink in. For so long she had hoped to trace her parents, find her identity, claim her true heritage. But she had never expected anything like this. Emotion swept over her, she felt her eyes fill with tears, her mouth tremble as she tried to speak. With a look of complete understanding, Gene took her in his arms and held her, while she put her head on his shoulders and wept.

"But I don't understand, Laurel. Why must you go?" Elaine Maynard's expression was a mixture of bewilderment and distress. "I've tried to make you comfortable here, assured you of my intention to support you at the Conservatory, provide you with anything you need —"

"I know, Grandmother, and I appreciate all you've done, all you want to do for me. But I have other plans now. Gene Michela and I are going to be married. He has been offered a position now at the Conservatory and will be well able to support me. I want to share this with my adoptive parents, have Gene meet them. We'll be married there in Meadowridge in November and then come back to live in Boston."

Mrs. Maynard shook her head as if not comprehending. "But, Laurel, I had it all planned, I intended — *wanted* you to make your home here with me until such time as you met some suitable young man. I planned to give you a reception to introduce you to people of our class, our kind —" Her words faded away as if she realized she was saying all the wrong things.

"Grandmother, it's not that I'm ungrateful. I know you have the best intentions in the world, but your plans are not my plans. We don't see alike, don't value the same things." Laurel spoke with quiet dignity. "I have found the person I love, the one with whom I want to spend the rest of my life. Gene Michela is everything I want, everything I've always hoped for, or need. When you get to know him better, you'll see I'm right. In fact —" Laurel leaned forward, looking intently into her grandmother's eyes. "I wanted to find my roots to satisfy my own longing to belong. Gene taught me to look for ways to give back what I already *have*. Both of us want you to be part of our life."

That sincere request seemed to touch a chord in a heart that had protected itself for years from feeling pain, regret, love. The long-suppressed vulnerability gave way. Speechless, Elaine Maynard held up her arms to her granddaughter. A minute later the fragile old woman was held in the young one's strong arms. Tears of forgiveness and reconciliation mingled on cheeks pressed close. Love withheld, love given, love renewed encompassed in a healing embrace.

Though outwardly reconciled to the inevitability of Laurel's leaving, as the time grew near for Laurel's departure for Meadowridge to prepare for her November wedding, Elaine Maynard's resistance to the idea stiffened. Laurel knew she had to somehow break through the wall her grandmother was building to shut out acceptance of Gene.

One Saturday evening in early October, she approached her. "Would you like to attend church with me tomorrow, Grandmother? Gene has been hired as soloist, and you've never heard him sing. I wish you'd come with me."

A shadow seemed to cross Mrs. Maynard's face and she turned away, visibly distressed.

"Is something wrong, Grandmother?" Laurel asked anxiously.

"It's just that — well, I haven't been . . . for a long time." She sighed. "Your grandfather was so bitter after . . . Lillian . . . we stopped going. Then when he was so ill and died, I felt God had —" her voice broke. Then, straightening her thin, elegant shoulders, she lifted her chin. "Yes, Laurel, perhaps that's what I *should* do, go back to church."

Sunday morning, looking regal in a gray, fur-trimmed coat and a feathered toque, accompanied by her granddaughter, Elaine Maynard took her place in the pew identified by a small brass plaque engraved with the MAYNARD family name.

It was a magnificent church, she thought, contemplating the stained-glass windows and, at the opening chords of the magnificent organ, she reminded herself that she and Bennett had contributed generously to its purchase. But when she heard the rich fullness of the tenor voice raised in worshipful praise, she knew *that* was the true contribution, the real gift.

She felt tremors coursing through her as the words of the first hymn resounded into the rafters: "All creatures of our God and King, lift up your voice and with us sing, Alleluia! Alleluia!" But it was when Gene sang the stirring lyrics of "It Is Well with My Soul" that Elaine was most deeply touched. Unexpectedly, the woman who had always prided herself on never publicly displaying emotion was moved to tears as the words reached the innermost places of her heart.

Believing no one was aware, she was surprised and comforted as Laurel's hand pressed hers. Looking at her grand-daughter, she smiled. *How blessed I am,* Elaine thought. *Thank You, Lord, for bringing her into my life — and the young man she loves. Forgive an old woman her past sins.* With a sigh of thankfulness, Elaine briefly closed her eyes, listening to the words of the hymn repeating them in her own heart: *Yes, it is well with my soul —*

23

Meadowridge was riotous with changing color — gold and russet and bronze — when Laurel returned just before Thanksgiving to await her wedding day.

Ava had insisted on commissioning Mrs. Danby to make the wedding gown and it hung now, a splendor of ivory lace and taffeta, in the closet of Laurel's old room. In fact, every moment since her homecoming had been filled brimful with preparations for the ceremony that would take place in the Community Church the week after Thanksgiving, not to mention plans for that most New England of all holidays. Ella had been cooking for days, eager to make a good impression on "Mr. Gene," and Jenny had come back to lend a hand with fall cleaning and polishing until the house fairly sparkled.

On Thanksgiving morning, when Gene was scheduled to arrive, Laurel insisted on going to the station by herself to meet him. A glance from Dr. Woodward stilled Ava's suggestion that they all go down in their newly acquired motor car to welcome Gene to Meadowridge, and Laurel set out on foot alone.

The yellow frame Meadowbridge train station was a nostalgic symbol to Laurel. Imprinted on her memory forever was the day she and the other orphans, shepherded by Mrs. Scott, were paraded out on the platform. Laurel remembered that shivery sensation inside, in spite of the fact that she was holding Toddy's hand on one side, Kit's on the other. Seeing it now, ten years later, brought all those feelings rushing back. Still, she knew she had been one of the lucky ones.

She thought also of the morning she had left Meadowridge to go to Boston, not sure she would ever come back. The empty heartsickness she had felt that misty morning gripped her as the slant-roofed station building came in sight.

But today there was not the slightest tinge of sadness in Laurel. Her step was as light as her heart, her pulses racing with excitement. Her anticipation mounted as she heard the train whistle in the distance. Clasping her hands tightly together, she moved to the edge of the platform peering down the tracks for the first sign of the engine rounding the bend. In her head she could hear the conductor's voice. "Meadowridge! Next stop, Meadowridge!"

And then she saw him, swinging down from the train's high step minutes after it had screeched to a stop, steam hissing, the grinding noise of steel against steel.

"Gene! Gene!" she called, waving her hand. She caught her breath as he came toward her, seeing his dark eyes sparkling and the smile that always made her heart turn over. Then she was swung up in his arms and she heard him whisper her name. Foolish tears gathered in her eyes as he set her back down on her feet.

"Let me look at you! These have been the longest weeks of my life!"

They said all the little, inconsequential things lovers say to each other, then Laurel gathered her wits about her enough to give directions to the baggage clerk to have Gene's luggage sent up to Meadowridge Inn where Dr. Woodward had made reservations for him.

"The house isn't far, so I thought we'd walk. I want to show you everything," she said almost shyly, hardly able to believe that he was really here with her in Meadowridge.

"It looks like I thought it would, only more so —" Gene remarked on the way. "Like everyone's dream 'hometown.'"

"Well, yes, maybe it does!"

As they strolled, hand in hand, Laurel realized she was seeing things with the long familiarity of childhood and Gene with fresh eyes. He marveled at the size of the elms, the willows on the sloping banks of the river when they crossed the arched stone bridge leading up to Main Street. The sun was out strongly now brightening the paint on all the houses along the way. Shining through the fretwork of gabled dormers, it cast lacy shadows on the clapboard. Autumn had been mild here, and most of the gardens still boasted flowers. Heavy-headed dahlias in various shades of orange, purple, yellow and white nodded in the brisk breeze.

Then finally they turned onto a winding lane with tall, arching trees and Laurel pointed to a white frame house with dark green shutters at the end.

"There it is." She smiled up at him. "Come on."

As they approached Gene saw a bunch of colorful Indian corn tied with wide yellow satin ribbon hanging on the front door that a minute later was flung open by a slender, dark-haired woman. Behind her stood a handsome, gray-haired man.

Laurel and Gene came up the porch steps together.

"Gene! How wonderful to meet you at last!" Ava said warmly and Dr. Woodward shook Gene's hand, saying, "Welcome . . . son."

Laurel felt tears again and her throat felt thick with emotion as she looked at these two she loved so dearly, then at the man she had chosen. A gladness surged up in her and a heartfelt prayer.

"Thank You, God, for all my blessings." The words of her favorite Psalm rushed into her mind, its beautiful words echoing in the fullness of her happiness: "Trust in the Lord, wait on him and he will bring it to pass. Trust him and he will give thee the secret desires of thy heart."

Dinner was served promptly at four. Jenny had come to help and could not seem to stop smiling as she served them. Every time she happened to catch Laurel's eye, which was often, she gave her a solemn wink.

Everything was perfect, Laurel thought, glancing to see if Gene appreciated Ava's artistry in arranging the table with its centerpiece of fruit and flowers — purple asters, marigolds combined with golden pears, and flame Tokay grapes. Her best Devonshire lace and linen cloth and napkins had been brought out, polished silver and glistening crystal, the good china that as a child Laurel had always admired — its design of the East Indian symbol of the Tree of Life in burnt orange and blue.

The food was a triumph of Ava and Ella's combined efforts. Ella herself brought in the turkey — golden brown, smelling deliciously, surrounded by tiny crabapples and parsley — then set it before Dr. Woodward with an air of deserved pride. This was followed by bowls mounded with snowy-white, light-as-air mashed potatoes, squash and creamed peas and pearl onions. Gravy boats were passed as well as numerous cut-glass containers of condiments — watermelon, pickles, peach chutney, quince jelly, and of course cranberry-orange relish. Two carafes of sweet apple cider were set at each end of the table to be poured into delicate, thin-stemmed goblets.

"Let us give thanks," Dr. Woodward said, bowing his head, holding out his hands to Laurel on his left and Gene on his right as was their custom. Ava completed the circle.

"Most gracious Father," he began. "We

are more aware than ever of Your unmerited favor, the many blessings You have lavishly given us. We thank You especially for our daughter, Laurel, and for the fine young man who will be her husband and our son. We thank You for the blessings of health, food and shelter, love of family and friends, and unwarranted bounty. We ask to be led by You in all things and be worthy to be called Your children. We ask this in the precious name of Your Son, Jesus Christ. Amen."

In a blur of happiness Laurel ate, not being entirely aware of what she tasted, filled as she was with a warmth and contentment that seemed to take up all the space within her, leaving very little for food. She looked at each of the people at the table, smilingly, silently loving them with a complete acceptance and gratitude.

Ava suggested they wait until later to have a choice of pie — pumpkin, apple or pecan — since everyone claimed they could not eat another bite just then. So taking their coffee the four of them went into the parlor.

It was getting dark outside with the quick falling darkness of an early winter day. The curtains were drawn, lamps lighted, and Dr. Woodward put a match to the fire that had been laid earlier. The kindling caught immediately with little snapping sounds, sending up spurts of bright flame. Soon a nicely burning fire glowed brightly in the hearth, reflecting on the brass fender and andirons in the shadowy room.

"Why don't you play for us, dear?" Ava suggested and Laurel took her place at the piano.

For a few minutes her fingers roamed the keyboard as if trying to find exactly the right melody for this special time. As she began to play a piece she knew was one of Dr. Woodward's favorites, her eyes circled the familiar room — the firelight burnishing the frames of the paintings, the polished furniture, the prisms of the candlesticks on the mantlepiece. Memories came flooding back — the first time she had seen this room, had discovered the piano, lifted its lid and let her fingers grope for the keys to play the simple little tune her mama had taught her years and years ago, guiding her tiny hands.

She played on, moving from one song to the other, an almost forgotten medley of music that the Woodwards most enjoyed. As her fingers moved across the keys, her mind wandered back and forth, in and out, everything coming together, past and present. All the varied experiences of her life, all the things that had happened began to take shape, form, fit into a whole.

As she played on, unconsciously a thrilling rightness of this moment she was sharing with the three people she loved most in the world swept over Laurel. All at once Laurel knew the joy of homecoming.

She had been on a lifelong journey to find her "real family," her "real home," and now she realized with a heart filled with understanding that her Heavenly Father had done "abundantly above all that we ask." He had given her more than one family and one home.

Sitting at the piano, in the comforting warmth of this familiar room, with the family He had provided for her, Laurel realized at last that she was no longer an orphan, but a lost child who had finally come home.